FRA FIDGET-KNICKERS

AND THE CHANCE TO GET EVEN

BY

COLIN WICKS

Illustrations by Su Wicks, and final proofs
edited by Dan McCloskey

The story and characters from this book are entirely made up from the author's imagination. He makes no apology for the fate that awaits Granddad Sprinkle-Tinkle inside this book.

First published in 2016 by CalviSu Publishing

ISBN 978-0-9935489-0-1

Website francesfidgetknickers.com

Text copyright © Colin Wicks 2016

Front cover illustrated by Su Wicks and coloured by Dan McCloskey.

Illustrations are the work of Colin Wicks, Su Wicks, and the final proofs edited by Dan McCloskey.

Colin Wicks asserts the moral right to be identified as the author, and Su Wicks, and Daniel McCloskey as the illustrators.

The people I should thank.

Here are the people I would like to thank, first of all, ME! Then there is my wife Su, who designed the front cover and Daniel McCloskey for colouring it in. Also ME again, as I did all the pictures inside the book, but my wife laughed so much because they were that bad I decided to sulk in the corner for a few hours. After which I asked Daniel McCloskey to re-draw them. I am still of the opinion that mine were better, but I am in the minority of one on that.

The proofreading was done by my wife Su, and my children, Nikhaela and Scott. The final editing and proofreading was done by Vicki Sennett of fool-proofs, and together with the artwork and corrections in spelling mistakes it has cost me an arm and a leg...so I am finding it difficult to get around on one leg, and it now takes me twice as long to type my stories into my computer with one arm...but it was worth the sacrifice...only kidding!

My picture of Mary Midget-Mouth...I'm a Picasso in the making!

Daniel McCloskey's picture of Mary Midget-Mouth...talentless effort in my opinion, but I was outvoted.

To my children, Nikhaela and Scott, whom this book was written for.

CHAPTER 1

MEET THE FAMILY

WELCOME
TO THE
VILLAGE OF

HEAD-BUTT-NO-BACON

There were whispers floating around the village of Head-Butt-No-Bacon. These rumours focused on Nutcracker Cottage, because the Knickers family who lived there were strange and very odd. Unknown to the villagers, the four occupants had been banished from a magical world and stripped of their magic. In the past, the Knickers family had done everything with just a wave of their magic wands. Slowly, over time, they had learnt to adjust to their new way of life without the help of any wizardry.

They all lived in an enchanted cottage with a thatched roof, and wooden windows painted white. Leading to the beautiful dwelling was a narrow dirt track with tall trees on either side. In between the oak and ash trees, wild berries ripened, their scent attracting an abundance of wildlife. Right at the very end of the dirt track stood a five-barred gate. Two thick posts held the gate in place, and it was easily opened by releasing a large metal latch.

Out of all four people living at number twenty-two
Nutcracker Cottage, there was only one person who could be
considered normal; this was Frances, who was currently
sitting at the breakfast table. Although only ten and slight of
build, with olive skin and long brown hair, she possessed the
mental ability of someone twice her age. You see, Frances
had acquired a fantastic memory, for she loved to read books
– lots and lots of them. This was just as well, for she needed
every drop of intelligence to keep herself from getting into
trouble. Having once had special magical powers, which she
had lost through no fault of her own, Frances had become
somewhat fidgety, and so her father had given his daughter
the pet name "Fidget".

Frances Fidget-Knickers watched some bees going about their business from the kitchen window, as her father Rupert, an unusual looking man, entered the room. He was tall and lean with a long, drawn-out face. Bridged over an even longer, drawn-out nose sat a pair of half-moon glasses. Due to his success as the top salesman at a self-moulding underwear factory, he'd decided to grow a moustache. At the end of every sale, he would twiddle both ends of his whiskers and then flick a pair of knickers into the air in celebration. The effects of this had caused him to be given the nickname Flicker, while both sides of his moustache now curled around like a tightly coiled spring. Everyone now called him Rupert Flicker-Knickers.

Mrs Wendy Knickers was completely the opposite, for she was extremely fat and very lazy. Being short, stout and twice the size of her husband, she considered herself to be above such things as working for a living. Food was really the only thing she cared for; large amounts of baked beans and boiled cabbage were particular favourites. This unfortunate mixture, however, had a very unpleasant effect on the woman's bowels. Unfortunately, for the rest of the household, Mrs Wendy Knickers spent most of her time lazing away the days slumped across a leather settee whilst blowing off. Instead of Wendy, everyone just called her Windy.

The oldest member of the household was Granddad Sprinkle-Tinkle, Mrs Windy-Knickers' father. This horrible man had been given the nickname Sprinkle, and there was a very good reason for this; the old man's aim was never true, and he always managed to give the toilet seat a good showering when going for a wee. Looking more like a skin-covered skeleton, with the complexion of a radish, he had the foulest temper known to anyone who had the misfortune of meeting him. It is quite possible that Granddad Sprinkle-Tinkle's extremely bad temper had caused his radish-like appearance.

CHAPTER 2

THE WINNING TICKETS

The day always started in the same manner, with all four sitting around the breakfast table while Rupert fretted.

"Blast! Blast! And hang them all!" he spluttered.

Frances watched her father.

Banging the table with one almighty blow, he exploded. "What shall I have for breakfast? Should I have toast? If so, should I have jam or marmalade on it? Maybe I'll have some cornflakes instead? What to drink ... a cup of tea ... with or without milk? Oh, blinking whatsits, it's too damned early in the morning for making such decisions!"

"Oh Rupert, you're not a morning person are you?" huffed Mrs Windy-Knickers. "What a fuss you always make over breakfast before going to work in the mornings."

"That I do," agreed Rupert, calming down. "What do you suggest I have, my little hippo?"

"Why don't you have one piece of toast with one half covered in jam and the other half covered in marmalade? After that, you could have a small bowl of cornflakes and two cups of tea, one with milk and the other without."

"By Heavens!" he cried out in delight, while placing the hot cup before him.

Frances kept watching. Her father lent forwards and, in doing so, his tie fell into the cup of steaming hot tea nestled underneath him.

"I can see why I married you, my darling. You're not just a pretty face; you've got the brains to go with it, my juicy, fat liver and onion faggot."

7

Stuffing a full slice of toast inside her mouth, the fat woman mumbled, "Now then, you old charmer, you know all the right things to say to a lady."

Granddad Sprinkle-Tinkle had spotted the tie sinking into the cup of his son-in-law's drink, and waited.

In keeping with her extremely bad manners, the lady of the house munched on. "Don't give me any of that smooth-talking lingo at this time in the morning."

Before he had time to answer, his wife brought up some wind and belched aloud, exposing the full contents of her mouth. Then she coughed, causing little pellets of food to shoot out.

Frances ducked for cover.

When her mother had finished spraying the table, she carried on with her words. "All that sweet-talking will do you no good, not when there's food to be eaten."

Just then, Granddad Sprinkle-Tinkle interrupted, pointing a long, bony finger at Rupert. "If you had half a brain, you'd be a wonder to medical science."

"Don't you start," Rupert began in retaliation, "or I'll come over there and squeeze that spot on the end of your nose. 'Whoosh' it will go, exploding like a volcano, leaving a big crater on the end of your face. That will put an end to your nose-picking days!"

"Calm down, you two – no good comes from fighting," puffed Mrs Windy-Knickers.

Frances decided to start her breakfast, while she kept on watching her mother.

Trying to regain her breath before another piece of toast was shovelled down her gullet, Mrs Windy-Knickers panted, "Make love, not war. And that's what I'm about to do to this delicious-looking morsel of food before me."

Mr Rupert Flicker-Knickers' attention had turned back to his wife. "That you are," he smiled, "and you do it so well."

Before the second piece was devoured, she told Rupert, "I think Father was trying to tell you about your tie. Kindly get it out of that cup. It won't do for a husband of mine to go around with tea stains on his clothes."

"Goodness me!" he cried out, grabbing the strip of material and wringing the liquid from it.

Knowing what was coming, Frances covered her ears. The air instantly filled with a squeal of pain.

"Ouch! Blinking hell! It's hot!" screamed her father.

"Of course it's hot," slurped his wife, from behind an upturned cereal bowl. "It comes from a hot place. What else would it be but hot?"

"Ouch, ouch, ouch!" squealed her husband.

Smacking her lips as the bowl was placed on the table, she turned to Frances and sighed, "Men – give them a brain and they'd be able to mess two things up at once!"

"Mummy," began Frances, politely. "You know you said if I was good you would let me have a friend over to stay for this weekend…"

Granddad Sprinkle-Tinkle sliced through the air and snarled at his granddaughter. "Don't you start troubling your mother! Can't you see she's got enough to do already, what with all those chocolate cakes and biscuits to eat after breakfast! Then there's twenty-five bags of crisps to get through before lunch!"

Instantly, Mrs Windy-Knickers gasped with a look of horror. "Only twenty-five, who's had the other fifteen packets?"

"I wouldn't put it past that nasty little oik of a daughter of yours," sniffed the old meanie in disgust.

"I haven't had them, and I've been really good this week, and I was looking forward to asking Mary Midget-Mouth over!" pleaded Frances.

After two more sniffs, the grandfather from hell grumbled. "No good will come from being friends with her. She's no good, rotten as they come. It makes me blood run cold and I'm getting goose bumps just thinking about it. But what else do you expect from someone who's uncouth, obnoxious and comes from the wrong side of town?"

"But Mary's father is a vicar!" stated Frances, in her friend's defence.

"Precisely my point," answered her grandfather. "I knew from the first time I set eyes on him that he was a troublemaker. So don't expect her to be coming over this weekend."

"That's just not fair," sulked Frances. "I never have anyone over to play with!"

"Hold your horses!" cried Rupert, turning towards Granddad Sprinkle-Tinkle. "Not so fast – let's not be too hasty about our little girl having a friend over for the weekend."

Frances Fidget-Knickers' ears pricked up.

"Remember what we agreed to, you old fool," snapped her father, yanking two pieces of paper from his pocket.

Frances tried to see what they were.

Mr Rupert Flicker-Knickers waved them. Then he bounced in his seat with joy. Turning to his wife, he yelped delightedly. "I've won! Can't you see? I've won the first prize in the raffle at work!"

Mrs Windy-Knickers took no notice as she busied herself with consuming more food.

Granddad Sprinkle-Tinkle sniffed a couple of times, uninterested with it all, and uttered, "Good for you."

Frances tried again to see what the papers were as they went waving about in her dad's hand.

Suddenly, the chair flew back, and up stood her father to do a little celebration dance, followed by a song.

"Look at these tickets.
Can't you see?
These beauties are for me!
All because I fiddled the raffle, fiddle de
dee!
If anyone complains, I'll give them the chop.
But if I'm in a good mood, I'll sack them on
the spot!"

"But Daddy, that's dishonest," gasped Frances, appalled.
"Shut up, you do-gooder!" snapped her grandfather. "Who
cares how dishonest and devious you have to be, as long as
you win – that's what really matters."
"Now then, Frances, no one likes a loser in this family,"
frowned her dad, as he encouraged his father-in-law to go
on. "She's got a lot to learn. Carry on, Granddad."
The lady of the house stopped eating and listened to her
father with great interest.

"In this family, I can dishonestly say you're going to come in second best," declared Granddad Sprinkle-Tinkle snootily. "You're on your way, my girl, to being a disgrace to this family. A ... dare I say it ... a person from the other side of town, like your friend, Mary."

"Quite right! Well spoken, Granddad," added Rupert.

A panicking scream filled the air as Mrs Windy-Knickers cried out. "Don't let it happen! Don't let my baby drift into a life of honesty!"

"Calm yourself," said her husband, briskly. "The little twerp will turn out just fine, or it's off to Mr Bone-Crunching's School for Disobedient Little Boys and Girls."

"I've heard about that school!" replied the mother, half asking. "That's the one, I think, where the headmaster gets hold of students and hangs them upside down if they step out of line? And throws them in the stocks?"

"That he does," agreed Rupert Flicker-Knickers.

"And whips them?"

"Of course."

"Until blood spurts out?"

"Every time."

"That's all right, then," sighed Mrs Windy-Knickers. "She can go. I feel much better now."

Seizing the opportunity, Rupert began. "In this family, when it comes to good fortune all I have to do is look at your mother, and I realise just how lucky I am. Straight A-grades, with stunning looks to boot. What more could a man want?"

"Oh Rupert, you old devil," giggled the large woman. "You are such a lucky chap."

BLOOD
WILL SPILL

Frances shuddered at the site that greeted her. Small streams of saliva trickled down her mum's chin. Pausing to wipe the slime away, Mrs Windy-Knickers proudly announced, "After all, you ended up with the beauty queen winner." Turning to Frances, she added, "Miss Piggy-Wiggy, you know, of the class for Hog Trotters for Young Ladies."

Frances stayed quiet as her insides kept shuddering.

Now her mother turned back to face Rupert as her curiosity took over, and asked, "By the way, what is the first prize?"

Mr Rupert Flicker-Knickers stood proudly at the head of the table and took in a deep breath, then he stated. "Before I start, I'll have no backchat from anyone."

"Oh, do get on with it," munched Mrs Windy-Knickers, finishing her third bowl of cornflakes.

"Certainly, my little oil tanker. Anything for you, my pet elephant," he beamed, gazing at her lovingly.

"Hurry up," gulped the fat woman, starting her fourth bowl of cereal.

Waving the tickets for all to see, he gabbled with excitement. "Look at these beauties – they're the winning tickets for a weekend away for two. I'm telling you, none other than a two-night stay over at the Shack-Em-Ups hotel in Snack-Pool!"

"Goodness me!" she spluttered.

Rupert gazed deep into his wife's eyes and said passionately, "Ah, my sumptuous rib-tickling porker, do you remember where we first met? Because I do, and you're as beautiful now as you were then, my sizzling lump of pork scratchings."

The huge woman took her fifth bowl of cornflakes and sprinkled a mountain of sugar over it. "How could I ever forget?" she replied.

"You never forget a thing, my lovely mammoth."

With that, she started to recite the story of their first meeting. "Well, it was like this. We first met in Snack-Pool many years ago, far too many years ago than I care to remember. Your friend, Rupert, you know – Freddy Shark-Breath. He arranged for us to meet on a blind date, just outside the pier."

"Good old Freddy fish-face," he smiled. "There's a friend I haven't seen in years."

"Do you mind? No interruptions, if you please," frowned Mrs Windy-Knickers, losing her train of thought. "Now, where was I?"

"Freddy Shark-Breath," chirped Frances Fidget-Knickers, jogging her mother's memory.

With no thanks forthcoming, Mrs Windy-Knickers snapped, "Don't you start with all these interruptions as well, young lady!"

Frances gave no response, as her mother went on. "Yes, I remember now. I was in complete control as always. It comes from many years of good breeding. But I could tell from a mile off that Rupert was a real bundle of nerves. Dear me, you got yourself into such a state! So much so, that you bent down to do up your shoelaces, and in doing so, ripped the backside out of your trousers. From crotch to waist, I might add. I really must admit, you cut quite a dashing sight with your underwear hanging out!"

While Frances giggled, her father gushed with pride and said, "My sweet apple dumpling, we'll walk along the very same pier again. Then we will pick ourselves up and dine on caviar and champagne. Because I've already phoned Mrs Bed-And-No-Breakfast's establishment and informed the good lady in question that we'll be on our way tomorrow. This time my trousers will stay in one piece!"

The huge woman fell back against her chair in shock. "Bless my soul!" she gasped.

Rupert, giving his wife no chance to recover, cried, "What a corker of a first prize, my delicious porker!"

Still in a daze, she mumbled, "Goodness me!"

Giving her very little time to gather her thoughts, he added, "It's for this weekend, my whopper of a pig's trotter!"

Shock turned to panic, and the bone-idle woman spluttered out a thousand questions. "But today's Thursday! What should I pack to take with us? What will I wear? There's not a thing in the house to eat! I'll have to do the shopping tonight instead of Saturday. Then there's a pile of ironing, which I might tell you is a mountain high, that still needs doing. What about all the washing up in the sink? Look at the house … it's a tip … it needs dusting and hoovering … and who's going to be doing that when we're away? Not me, that's for sure!" The last and most important thing that spluttered from her lips was, "Who's going to look after Frances?"

"Don't panic, my little diesel engine," smiled Rupert. "I've arranged for Granddad to look after her. He doesn't mind if a friend comes over. As for the shopping, we can phone through to the supermarket and get them to deliver. We can arrange for a cleaner to come in. I'll leave some money with your father to pay for the cleaning. Because, bright and early tomorrow morning, we'll be on our way to paradise!"

Frances Fidget-Knickers' thoughts turned to revenge, as she watched her father dance even more merrily than before.

Rupert Flicker-Knickers patted his back pocket. "I have the travel permits right here!"

Trembling with eagerness, Mrs Windy-Knickers asked her father. "Are you sure?" Before he had a chance to answer, she asked again. "Do you mind?"

The old man stopped what he was doing and glared at his granddaughter. With a sniff, he growled in a low and menacing voice, "I'll have no foolish nonsense out of you or your friend. Any monkey business and you'll both be in for the chop."

Frances stared back with angel eyes that disguised the lie behind them, and said innocently, "Me? I'll be as good as gold. And you won't get any trouble out of Mary, either."

CHAPTER 3

FUSSING

Mary Midget-Mouth, a skinny little girl with mousy brown hair tied in a ponytail, had been dropped off bright and early. She jumped on the end of her friend's bed, literally bouncing with excitement, and asked, "What are we going to do?"

"Well, we're going to make my grandfather wish he had never been born," answered Frances.

"You must really hate him?"

"I wouldn't mind if he was like normal grandparents. At least they are kind, gentle, loving and generous … which he is not. Instead, I get the world's worst grandfather. Who just so happens to be grumpy, ill-natured and very mean."

"He's all of those things and more," agreed Mary. "Has he always been like this?"

Frances began to recall how her grandfather had got them all banished. "You know our secret? The one you promised to never tell?"

Her friend looked slightly awkward and her cheeks flushed. "Oops!"

"Mary," cringed Frances, tensely. "Who have you told?"

Cheeks glowing from the embarrassing moment, she answered, "Only my father. It just slipped out. You know, about you being banished from a magical world. And how you had all lost your powers because they'd been taken away, but House still possessed its ability to perform magic."

"For God's sake!" stressed Frances Fidget-Knickers. "I'm dead meat now!"

"Don't worry."

"But it's not you getting burned at the stake for being a witch!" Frances shuddered, nervously.

"Don't worry," said Mary, for the second time. "He put it all down to my fertile imagination and too many E numbers."

"So he suspects nothing?"

Mary's cheeks faded, as her answer put to rest the awkward feeling. "Not a thing," she winked.

"Thank God for that!" replied Frances with a sigh. And she continued telling her story. "It was from the age of two that I first began to notice how very beastly my grandfather was."

"As young as that?" Mary asked, preventing her friend from going on.

Frances thought, and the tiny brain receptors instantly came back with, "Yes, my head was growing and swelling with intelligence from an early age."

"You're the cleverest person I know," smiled Mary, approvingly. "Even more than my father, and he went to university."

"I don't think I'm that clever."

"Wrong!" cried Mary insistently, remembering something from school.

"I beg your pardon?" blinked Frances, a little surprised.

"I overheard Mr Sketch-It, the art teacher, talking at school last week."

"Who was he talking to?"

"Miss Leg-It, the games teacher."

"What about?" asked Frances.

"You."

"What did he have to say about me?"

"Actually, both of them had quite a lot to say."

"Come on, out with it then!"

Mary went into a full-blown stage performance and mimicked the two teachers. In a deep voice, she spoke, "Frances Fidget-Knickers' knowledge is quite outstanding, Miss Leg-it. A very gifted child indeed, far above her years."

Frances enjoyed the acting. "That's just like him."

In a softer voice, Mary said, "I know what you mean, a very exceptional young girl. Truly remarkable and highly educated for someone so young."

"That sounds just like her," giggled Frances.

Now back to the deeper voice of Mr Sketch-It, Mary went on, "Her parents must be academics, or pay for home tutoring."

"They got that wrong," insisted Frances. "I've done it all on my own."

In a higher voice, Mary finished, "How very kind of her parents to take the time to invest in her future. She must have such pleasant memories – what a lucky girl she is."

Frances Fidget-Knickers let out a deep sigh. "If only they knew. Unfortunately, my memories are the worst."

"I have such lovely thoughts of my mother and father," smiled Mary, recalling them. "Nice holidays away, for starters. Then there's my grandparents – my grandfather does really silly things. He doesn't mean to, but it makes my grandmother really cross."

"No such luck for me," said Frances, spurting out her past. "For eight years longer than I care for, I've had to be polite, respectful and considerate."

Mary raised her eyebrows and calculated the amount of time, "Seeing as you are only ten, that's eighty per cent of your life."

"Yes it is, and for eight years all I can remember is my grandfather's wicked, spiteful and horrid ways."

This was a little unsettling, as Mary Midget-Mouth asked, "Time for a bit of revenge, then?"

"Until now, there's never been a time good enough for springing my traps."

"Why's that?"

"The only time I ever have for such trickery is at the weekend," she answered.

"What stopped you?"

"Weekends always meant that one of my parents would be at home," said Frances, as her eyes lit up brightly. "So far, he has escaped my childish scorn."

"Not for long," smiled Mary, relaxing her eyebrows.

"Just as well," frowned Frances Fidget-Knickers. "For a woman's scornfulness is a mighty powerful thing. You see, they become scorpions with nasty stings in their tails."

"Goodness, I must remember never to upset you," gulped Mary, jokingly.

Frances Fidget-Knickers' eyes opened wide, so wide that they nearly popped out. "Although I possess a caring attitude, I still have urges for revenge flowing through my veins. So now is the time for planning our attack."

"How are we going to defeat him?" asked Mary. "He's so much bigger and uglier than us."

"So he's bigger, and most definitely uglier than we are," smiled Frances, while nodding her head. "But we have the one thing he does not."

21

All this time Mary had been bouncing about on her friend's bed. Now she sat down and scratched her head. As she did so, two questions popped out. "Do we? What's that, then?"

"Intelligence," beamed Frances enthusiastically. "There will be no casualties on our side. We will be crusaders and charge into battle like the cavalry – with crushing blows from our swords, we will strike down the enemy and return victorious."

"Like the knights of old, a fight for truth and justice," Mary said excitedly.

A thunderous boom of annoyance shot across the hall before Frances had a chance to reply.

"Whatever is that all about?" asked Mary Midget-Mouth.

Frances shrugged her shoulders, and replied, "It sounds like my dad is having problems."

"Blast! Blast! And hang them all!" screamed Rupert Flicker-Knickers.

"Yep, I was right."

Both girls ran over to see what all the fuss was about. In the master bedroom, on the bed, sat a large, light blue suitcase, packed almost to bursting point. Mrs Windy-Knickers carelessly tossed more and more clothes into it. Another piece of luggage, the same size and colour, sat on the bedroom floor, with Mr Rupert Flicker-Knickers having all sorts of problems.

Frances and Mary stood in the doorway watching.

The strain on Rupert's face was making him more and more angry, until he exploded once more. "Blast! Blast! And hang them all!"

Mrs Windy-Knickers just tutted as a few items went into her handbag.

Still struggling like crazy her husband yelled out in a thundering temper, "I'm going to hit this thing with a mallet!"

Then he stood up.

His wife ignored the standing moment, and carried on with her packing.

Rupert desperately worked away as his temper took over. In silence the suitcase got a swift kick.

Peeling off clothes from several hangers and wedging them into the travelling case perched on top of the bed, Mrs Windy-Knickers huffed, "Oh Rupert, you should think of your blood pressure!"

Dropping to his knees frantically trying to pin down the suitcase, he looked up with a face as hot as the sun. "Hang them all!" he cursed.

In a swaying motion, the lady of the house waddled over to her husband, plonked herself down on the rectangular piece of luggage, and wheezed a chesty wheeze. "That temper is going to get the better of you one day."

"Ha ha! Got you now, you little blighter!" cried Rupert brightly, flicking the catch down.

"Better?"

Having nothing but praise for his wife, he said, "That's just what it needed, my enormous chocolate drop. What a clever so-and-so you are."

Her lungs inhaled a deep breath of air, and out popped her chest. "Brains, not brawn," Mrs Windy-Knickers exclaimed. "That's what was needed, and it's lucky for you that I've got the full package."

"By Heavens, that you are!" smiled Rupert. "My colossal dumpling, to me you have the qualities of womanhood like no other."

The repulsive lady fluttered her eyelashes. "Do I?" she asked, lifting her stomach.

"My ginormous whopper of a shocker," beamed Rupert, grinning like a Cheshire cat. "You're the whopper of a shocker I've always dreamed of."

"Stop teasing me," she laughed, letting go of the fat around her middle. It fell over her chubby legs.

"My dear thunder thighs, there's no one luckier than me."

"I suppose not – after all, you'd probably still be struggling with this suitcase," nodded the fat woman.

"Ha, my wonderful plump lump," he sighed, as his attention turned to the journey ahead. "Shall we depart and swoon the weekend away, my voluptuous rump of blubber?"

All this time, the two girls standing in the doorway had not been noticed.

"First I want to check on Frances and her friend," she answered, uncharacteristically.

"Fiddling fiddle sticks!" he cried out impatiently. "Can't we leave them to their own devices and just go?"

24

The huge woman wobbled for a moment and regained her true self. "I don't know what came over me. Best we get going, then."

Searching for the other suitcase, Rupert looked over to the door and spotted the two girls. "Right, you two can stay out of the way because we're off in a minute."

"And be quiet while you're about it," added Mrs Windy-Knickers.

Not wanting to be disciplined, the two girls made themselves scarce and sat halfway down the stairs.

Inside the bedroom the sounds of unrecognizable whispers floated out of the door. Half a minute later, two overfilled suitcases, looking like they were about to explode, had been dragged to the top of the landing.

"What have you put in these things?" gasped Rupert.

In less than two shakes of a lamb's tail, Mrs Windy-Knickers passed her husband. Frances shook her head at the embarrassing moment that greeted her eyes. The fat woman looked even more ridiculous than ever, wearing all her clothes three sizes too small, as she huffed, "It's very important for a lady of my curvaceous stature – and, not forgetting, elegance – to keep her physique in tip-top condition."

"That it is, my whopper," beamed Rupert Flicker-Knickers, his smile straining under the load.

"So I've loaded them up with some snacks for the journey," she insisted. "After all, I don't want to end up looking like a twig."

"That will never do, my shocker," gasped her husband.

"Rupert, will you hurry up and get those suitcases in the car," puffed the huge woman. "I don't want to be standing around here all day."

Rupert Flicker-Knickers quickly picked up the extremely heavy luggage. Gasping under the weight, his legs began to bend and buckle. "Blimey, you sure you haven't packed the kitchen sink?"

Frances and Mary watched him struggle.

Suddenly, after taking only his very first step, Rupert lost control. "Gawd help us!"

For the two girls, it was fun to carry on watching. "Take cover," giggled Frances.

Like a pinball, Rupert bounced from side to side all the way down the stairs, only just managing enough time to say to the two girls on the way past, "Lumps and bumps everywhere, it's just like trying to wrestle my wife!"

As Rupert Flicker-Knickers finally disappeared outside the front door, there came grunting and groaning noises. "We're only going for the weekend and not the week!" Then everyone heard sounds of lifting. "Heave-ho!" echoed out, as the travelling cases went clunk, clonk and bonk. Once they had been loaded into the car waiting outside, Rupert called out in a softer tone, "Hurry up, my lovely Piggy Wiggy. Shall we be on our way?"

Hearing the car boot slam shut, the fat woman announced, "Right, we're off."

"Have a nice time!" smiled Frances, waving her goodbye.

Waddling to the bottom of the stairs, her mother replied, "No pinching my chocolates." Just before she disappeared through the front door, she added, "I'll know if you have."

All the two girls heard was the sound of a whining engine straining under the weight as they sped away.

Instantaneously, Granddad Sprinkle-Tinkle shouted, "What's all that noise out there, disturbing me sleep?"

Frances and Mary froze.

"What time do you call this?" he grumbled some more. "Right, someone is in for the chop!"

There was nowhere to go and nowhere to hide.

Swiftly, and with the sound of shuffling slippers, Granddad Sprinkle-Tinkle appeared at the top of the stairs.

He looked down at them.

Looking up, Frances and Mary saw the most awful sight.

Unlike their clean clothes, he was wearing a pair of stained trousers and a moth-eaten shirt. Then the old man began to grumble. "There you are, you blasted bag of bones. And who is that nasty little whippersnapper with you?"

"This is Mary," answered Frances.

"Is it, now?" grumbled Granddad Sprinkle-Tinkle, taking menacing steps towards them. "We've met before?"

"Yes."

"So, Mary, what time do you call this, then?"

Checking her wristwatch, she answered, "Ten o'clock."

"I don't think you are telling me the truth, young lady."

"But it is ten o'clock," insisted Mary.

"Don't take that tone of voice with me," said Granddad Sprinkle-Tinkle, cantankerously.

Mary stood her ground.

Now trying to pick a fight, he continued, "As I said, it couldn't possibly be ten o'clock, because I have never seen two tens in the same day. I know this to be true, for I'm never normally awake at this unearthly hour."

"Take a look at my watch and see for yourself, if you don't believe me," she said, presenting her arm.

The old man grabbed Mary's arm and twisted it slightly.

"Ouch!" she whimpered.

"Shut up, you little weed," hissed the wretched old man, "or I'll rip it off."

Mary held her tongue.

The old man inspected the wristwatch. "See! What did I tell you? There is no sign of two tens on this watch anywhere. Take a look for yourself."

Glancing quickly at her wrist, she yelped, "No, there isn't."

With another little twist of Mary's arm, he asked, "So who is right then?"

"You are," she winced, giving in to the pain.

"I can't hear you," smiled Granddad Sprinkle-Tinkle nastily, turning her arm until it wouldn't turn anymore.

"You are!" she repeated.

Somehow, the old pimple-head managed to force Mary up onto her toes, as he stressed, "You will do as I say, or else!"

"Okay," she yelped.

Granddad Sprinkle-Tinkle let go of the twisted limb and swivelled around to face his granddaughter. "And what I say goes, make no mistake about that."

Fearing the worst, Frances just nodded.

"Well, child," moaned the horrid blister of a grandfather, "where's me mug of tea?"

From experience, she had learned not to provoke him while he was in such a foul mood.

"Come on, you ungrateful little girl," snapped Granddad Sprinkle-Tinkle. "Go and make me drink. Don't you go forgetting that I like ten dessertspoons of lovely white sugar! I also like it piping hot so I can smell the sweetness of the granules. Don't forget to put it on a saucer, because as you know I like to tip me tea on to the saucer and sip it out. And a teaspoon – don't you dare bring in me tea without one. I'll be waiting in the front room, where I will be sitting in me rocking chair. That reminds me, I do hope the sun is not out – nothing worse than a sunny day. What we need is more rain! It would be much easier to watch you two if it rains all weekend."

"But Granddad," gasped Frances, "isn't all that sugar bad for your teeth?"

"Nonsense, child," said the nastiest grandfather sharply. "Who's been filling your head with rubbish like that?"

"My dentist, Mr Tooth-Cracker, told me."

The old man sniggered. "With a name like that, I'm not surprised."

"He's a very good dentist, Granddad."

"Good dentist or not," sniffed Granddad Sprinkle-Tinkle, "I can tell you he is one hundred per cent wrong."

"How?" asked Frances Fidget-Knickers.

Now the old bag of bones stood up as straight as he could, and proudly stated. "It's quite simple, because I've been having ten sugars in me drinks since I was born, and I've never needed to see a dentist once in all that time."

"You've never been to the dentist?" gasped Frances.

"No, never, and I still have a full set of teeth without a single filling."

"Really?" said Mary.

"Not one filling?" Frances asked.

Granddad Sprinkle-Tinkle's bent down and opened his mouth. Frances and Mary peered in. Inside the disgusting opening, a mouthful of mangled, twisted, decaying teeth dripped with fungi. "There you go," he gurgled.

"Oh," they answered awkwardly.

With a snap, the horrid mouth was closed. "See?" he grumbled, regaining his posture. "What did I tell you? Simply perfect. So don't go telling me lies. Be off with you, before I lose me temper, you spoilt little brats."

Frances and Mary did exactly that and went off to the kitchen, where the experiment of revenge was about to begin.

CHAPTER 4

MUG OF TEA

The huge white kitchen was spotless. Not a single crumb or speck of dust could be seen. Slate-coloured worktops and matching floor broke the whiteness. Sitting on the worktops, everything was in its place and made from stainless steel.

Frances Fidget-Knickers entered first, followed by Mary Midget-Mouth.

"Look at the size of this place," gasped Mary in amazement. "And it's so beautiful! It wasn't like this the last time I came over."

The next moment, the house shook ever so gently and a deep, kind, softly spoken voice sounded out from nowhere. "THANK YOU," shuddered the cottage, kindly. "I'VE REDECORATED. DO YOU LIKE IT?"

"It's fantastic!" exclaimed Mary, looking up to the ceiling.

"YOU SHOULD VISIT MORE OFTEN," replied House.

She smiled. "I will, thank you, House."

"Looks like you've made a friend," Frances said.

"At least someone likes me," she sniffed, making her nose wrinkle up in a pleasing way.

"How's your arm?"

The arm-twisting still lodged firmly in her mind, Mary's facial expression changed to a fighting face. "It really hurts. If only I was bigger, I'd punch him on the nose."

"Let's not use senseless violence," insisted Frances, beaming. "We're going to have much more fun than that."

Rubbing her arm, Mary winced, "It would make me feel better, it does ache."

"I know the last time you came over he did some very nasty things to you."

"He certainly did," shuddered Mary. "Like putting my fingers in the plug socket and turning on the power. I couldn't do a thing with my hair afterwards. For weeks I walked around looking like I'd just seen a ghost."

"I remember," laughed Frances, searching through the cupboards. "Luckily for you, he wasn't in a bad mood that day."

"My mum, she wouldn't believe me when I told her," insisted Mary. "She said I was making it up, and if I kept telling lies, I'd have to explain myself to my father."

"That's the problem with grown-ups," declared Frances, with her head still inside a cupboard. "They just don't take the time to listen."

"You're dead right there."

"Never mind, at least we have this opportunity to delve deeper into our minds and explore the darkest depths of getting even."

"You sound just like Mr Trickery, the drama teacher," frowned Mary, not fully understanding.

"No acting here, if you please," smiled Frances, thoughtfully. "I don't know about you, but my brain is fizzing like crazy. Ideas just keep popping into my head. I have the beginnings of revenge frothing to the surface, ready for experimentation."

"What do you have in mind?" asked Mary eagerly.

"First," chirped Frances Fidget-Knickers, who was now looking under the sink, "we have to remember the old fossil is a hundred times older than us, and then there is that temper of his."

"Are you scared? Because I am!" Mary asked.

"A little," answered Frances instantly. "If we are going to succeed, it would be better to be a little frightened, because it helps to keep us on our toes."

"I'm a very fast runner."

"I didn't mean that, it was just a figure of speech."

"Oh, I see. Now you're sounding like my dad."

Still rummaging under the sink, Frances asked, "You're not backing out, are you?"

Mary stood her ground. "No way!" she said sternly. "Frances, what are you looking for?"

"Something my mum takes for constipation," replied her friend, moving things aside.

"What's constipation?"

"My mum's a bit sluggish with her bowels at times."

"What?"

"She finds it hard to poo!"

"Oh, I see," smirked Mary. "Have you found it?"

"It's not here. It must be upstairs in my mum's room. Come on, follow me!"

Mary could not understand why they were off down the garden path instead of going upstairs to Mrs Windy-Knickers' bedroom. "Where are we going?"

As Frances skipped and hopped down the garden path and into the garage, she answered, "Firstly, if this trick is to have the maximum impact, I will need a screwdriver."

"Why?"

"Wait and see!"

The garage was full of hand-held implements, stacked neatly in lines along the garage walls. Each tool hung by a piece of string, threaded through tiny holes and looped over nails fixed to the internal brickwork. To the right, there was a shovel, fork, rake and yard broom. To the left hung hammers of all kinds and sizes, saws of many descriptions, pliers for all uses and screwdrivers for all sorts of jobs. Right at the very far end sat an old, rusting lawnmower. Frances headed for the rack of screwdrivers. Scanning them, she took a small one with a cross-shaped head. It fitted neatly into her jeans pocket without showing.

"Come on, follow me!" Frances said in haste.

Retracing their steps back up the garden path and through the back door, they stopped just before the bottom of the stairs. In the front room, they heard Granddad Sprinkle-Tinkle reading aloud.

"Secondly, find a corkscrew. Not the modern type, but the good old-fashioned ones with a solid wooden handle. Having already selected your victim, begin to screw the implement into the person's ear. As you go deeper into the inner ear, this will have the desired effect, causing excruciating pain. In doing so, it will make the victim's eyes widen and water as the corkscrew goes further into the skull."

There was a slight pause, and then Granddad Sprinkle-Tinkle ended with, "Now that's what I call a very good book."

Frances turned to look at Mary. "Best we don't get caught. Follow me, and be careful because the stairs are a bit creaky."

With a hesitant first step, Mary followed behind, suddenly stopping dead in her tracks as a stair let out a nasty creaking noise.

"Sssh!" whispered Frances.

Both of them stood perfectly still. They listened for Granddad Sprinkle-Tinkles' booming shout. The air was filled with tension, but the old man didn't say a word.

Frances looked at Mary and whispered again. "Why is it, when you need to keep a secret – and I mean a super huge one – that these stairs want to give the game away?"

"You're darn right about that," Mary Midget-Mouth whispered back.

"It's just as well that I'm experienced in these matters. I can remember where all the creaky ones are. Just follow in my footsteps," pointed Frances, showing her friend where not to step.

But even with the controlled and steady steps, there came a cracking noise from Mary's toe bones. The sound was made so much worse by the emptiness of the hallway.

"Be quiet!" Mary stressed to her foot, tensely. "We'll end up getting caught, and I don't fancy a corkscrew in my ear, so behave!"

Frances giggled silently, and they both made their way to Mrs Windy-Knickers' bedroom. One particular bottle on the dressing table seemed to gleam unknowingly at Mary.

Frances Fidget-Knickers' hands weaved in and out of the many different objects scattered over the surface. "Here they are," she declared finally, picking up a brown bottle.

Inside there was movement. "What are they?" Mary asked, watching them wriggle.

"These are for when you get a blocked tummy – they're called Slug Busters."

"So that's what they look like," muttered Mary, inspecting the bottle. "I've never seen anything like them before."

"They might look like slugs. And feel like slugs. That's because they are slugs." insisted Frances, knowledgeably.

"And she eats them?"

"No, you take them with a drink. They help with my mother's bowel movements, when she gets a bit bunged up inside."

Inquisitively, Mary asked, "Will they kill him? I do hope so!"

Frances Fidget-Knickers gasped. "We don't want that!"

Mary made the sign of the cross with her right hand, from forehead to chest, and from shoulder to shoulder. "Dear God, forgive me for my sins and for the wicked thoughts." Looking up, she continued, "If you could see it in your heart, please let this trick leave him in severe pain and discomfort." Turning to her friend, she finished, "Amen."

Unscrewing the top, Frances shook the bottle carefully. Out fell eight shell-less creatures onto the palm of her hand. Then she said in a witch-like voice, "They glisten with demons! They shine with evil spirits! May these eight foul serpents call the Prince of Darkness to do our work!"

"Blimey, you're good at that," smiled Mary.

"Why, thank you," beamed Frances Fidget-Knickers, shaking the hand with the slugs inside.

"Shouldn't we just use one?" Mary asked, not really wanting to kill the old tyrant. "Just to see how it goes?"

"The way I look at it is like this," Frances began to explain, in her normal voice. "One slug takes around two hours before it starts to work on my mother. So if we give my grandfather eight of these beauties, then it should work eight times faster."

"How do you work that out?"

Enthusiastically, Frances began to do her sums and muttered aloud. "Now, let's see if I've got my sums right. Two hours equals one hundred and twenty minutes."

"Correct."

"One slug takes one hundred and twenty minutes before it starts to work."

"If you say so."

"Eight slugs should work eight times faster."

"I'm getting a bit lost."

"So divide eight into one hundred and twenty."

"Now I am lost."

"You get fifteen minutes exactly," Frances said excitedly, looking at Mary.

"Do you?"

"There, you see – quite simple, really."

"My head hurts," she sighed.

Feeling pleased with her arithmetic, and clutching the Slug Busters tightly, Frances Fidget-Knickers hurried to the toilet. In front of the door, she bent down and handed Mary the slugs. Taking the screwdriver out of her pocket, she began to turn the screws – the very same screws that held the toilet door handle in place.

Unexpectedly, there came a booming shout from downstairs, which made the pair of them jump.

"Where's me cup of tea? You made that drink yet?" protested Granddad Sprinkle-Tinkle. "I'm dying of thirst in here! And that's only going to make me meaner and even more bad-tempered!"

Apprehensively, Frances looked at Mary. "There's not much time – I'll have to work faster," she said, worried.

"If I have to get out of this chair..." roared Granddad Sprinkle-Tinkle.

Cutting her grandfather short, Frances shouted, "I just have to go to the toilet first."

"Make sure you wash your hands!" said the old man, sternly. "And if you're not here with a mug of tea in the next ten minutes, and not a second later, I'm going to use this corkscrew on you. Maybe a little ear wax-pulling might help to sort you out!"

Mary shuddered. "Do you think he means what I think he means?"

"Afraid so – and I wish he would stop moaning!" Frances frowned, annoyed.

Mary watched Frances getting to work on the job at hand. "I'm sure I've missed something," she said, pondering.

Still concentrating on the task in front of her, Frances insisted, "Wouldn't it be bliss if he never said another word? And I do mean never!"

"I just cannot put my finger on it," puzzled Mary.

Turning her mind fully to adjusting the screwdriver, Frances muttered away. "Why do screws come in all different shapes and sizes?"

Mary watched, a little baffled, but said nothing.

"I suppose these slender-shaped things are very useful," she grinned, mischievously. "They fix and fasten lots of objects together. Such as cupboards onto walls, hinges onto doors, doors onto doorframes. And, of course, handles onto toilet doors."

There was a sudden spark of light inside Mary's head. "Clever – now I see what you're up to."

With the biggest grin of all, Frances Fidget-Knickers chuckled. "When you have a turd buster escaping from your rear end, and when you can't hold onto it any longer, a door handle would come in mighty useful if you needed to go to the toilet in a hurry."

Mary Midget-Mouth and Frances both burst into a muffled fit of laughter and slammed each other's hands, palm against palm, as though a small victory had already been won.

It soon stopped, as it dawned on Mary that the missing thought had just popped into her head. "The door – it opens the wrong way! Why didn't I think of it before? We've just wasted all that time and effort for nothing."

Brightly, Frances answered with great pleasure, "My dad had to change this one. It opens outwards. Because it's such a small room, my mother just couldn't fit inside with the door working the other way."

Mary's chest eased a little from the pounding beats of her heart, and she sighed, "For a moment there, I thought we'd messed up big time."

"Not so," Frances smiled, unwinding the screws that held the door handle in place. "Let's see. Not too loose. Not too tight … feels just about right to me. Stage one of the plan is complete."

Popping the screwdriver back into her pocket, the two girls got an ear shocker. "Smackings – that's what you will be getting if you don't hurry up with me drink!" shrieked Granddad Sprinkle-Tinkle.

"Not to worry, Granddad!" shouted Frances.

"And your friend!" he bellowed back.

Winking at Mary to follow her, both girls ran down the stairs. In the same tone, she shouted again, "I've just finished, and I've washed my hands, like you said!"

"Seven more minutes and I will be doing some ear wax-pulling!" the old man snapped back.

Sliding across the kitchen floor, Frances grabbed the kettle as she went by, and stopped in front of the sink. Then, quickly filling the kettle up, sliding back, plugging it in and grabbing her grandfather's mug, she pirouetted to a halt.

"Ten out of ten for style," Mary gasped, in her best judging voice. "And full marks for effort."

With a circling wave of her hand, she curtsied. "Thank you, all my many adoring fans."

GRANDDAD'S MUG

The milk, tea bag and sugar – all ten dessertspoonfuls – were in the mug just as the kettle finished boiling. Carefully, Frances took the slugs from Mary and dropped all eight in the mug. Then she poured in the steaming water until the mug was filled. They both watched the misty vapour rise as the tea bag half sunk into a sea of evilness, along with the slugs.

"Excellent!" exclaimed Mary. As the mist of steam rose, and wonderment filled her eyes, she said, "Looks like a devil's poison. Will it work?"

"Only one way to find out," beamed Frances.

Taking the tea bag out and throwing it away, Frances Fidget-Knickers carried the mug out of the kitchen, looking very odd sat on top of a saucer.

"I'm not saying a word if I can help it," winced Mary, rolling her shoulder. "My arm's only just stopped hurting."

Without spilling a single drop, they made their way into the front room and presented the mug to Granddad Sprinkle-Tinkle.

"Here you are, Granddad," she smiled, quickly adding, "Mummy said things might taste a little bit strange this week – something about not having the right brand of sugar at the supermarket,"

"Poppycock, child," grunted her nasty grandfather, looking out of the window.

"It's true," insisted Frances.

Sitting in his rocking chair, he moaned, "Rain, why doesn't it ever rain when you want it to?"

Both girls stood perfectly still.

Next thing they knew, he had turned to face them both. "You two – excuses worked out already, I suppose?" he asked, and then he looked back up at the sky in silence.

Giving up on the idea of not saying anything, Mary made her statement. "Frances really needed the toilet. I could have made it, but I don't know where you keep all the things to make a cup of tea."

From the back or his head, he moaned. "All I ever get is blasted excuses! If you can't make a decent mug of tea, then say so. In that way, you'd stop wasting me time, and I could get on with giving you both a damned good flogging."

Mary's insides went all a-flutter. It was as though a thousand butterflies were flying around inside her stomach.

Frances cautiously stood her ground. "But it's true what Mary said. And if you don't believe me about the shopping, you can check with Mummy when she comes home. The man who delivered it from the supermarket said he got some things wrong."

Very quickly, the grizzly old man looked back at them and then out of the window again. The sagging folds of skin under Granddad Sprinkle-Tinkle's jaw shook uncontrollably. "Don't think that I won't be checking, because it sounds like a load of old cobblers to me."

"Here, Granddad, here's your mug of tea," Frances said, presenting the drink once more. "I'm sure she will tell you the same as I just did. Look, I remembered the teaspoon. The mug is on a saucer, just the way you like it."

A bony hand stretched out and snatched the drink. With the free hand, he whirled the teaspoon around inside the mug until it was going so fast he lost control. It made an awful clanging noise. Unnaturally, Granddad Sprinkle-Tinkle smiled. "Music to me ears," he hissed.

The two girls cringed awkwardly.

Raising himself up, in a slithering movement, he hissed once more. "There'd better be ten heaps of sugar in it? Good size ones, I might add."

"Yes, there are, I made sure of it," Frances answered. With great skill, she changed the subject. "Can we go and get some colouring pencils?"

"No good without a book," sniffed Granddad Sprinkle-Tinkle, his nose half hanging over the mug.

"Of course, Granddad."

With a glance over to where Mary was standing, and with teasing contempt, he grinned, "I can smell if there's not enough sugar in me tea. And you know what that means, don't you?"

Mary nodded her head, as if to say yes, and remained silent.

With the bitterness of a freezing cold day, Granddad Sprinkle-Tinkle spoke chillingly. "I'm only waiting for one of you to make a mistake. Because it will give me the excuse I need. I particularly like the thought of poking a coat hanger up your nose and seeing if I can wiggle out some brains."

Not exactly shocked by this, Frances Fidget-Knickers continued, "Can we please get some colouring pencils?"

"For Heaven's sake, girly!" he barked fiercely. "What is it now?"

"Granddad," began Frances, her plan to watch the trick starting to unfold, "can we sit at the dining table?"

More interested in the drink, Granddad Sprinkle-Tinkle slurped, "Be off with you and leave me alone. Don't expect me to clean up after you. I'm a babysitter, not a blinking housemaid!"

Frances, a look of excitement swelling in her face, hooked Mary's arm and they both flew from the room.

CHAPTER 5

WOULD IT WORK?

During the next thirty minutes, Frances Fidget-Knickers and Mary Midget-Mouth collected up two colouring books and a tin of colouring pencils, and made up a little song. Rehearsed and ready for a performance, they sang it.

"What do you do, if you want to do a poo,
In an English country garden?
Pull down your pants, and fertilize the plants,
In an English country garden.
Watch out for the ants, they'll crawl inside your pants,
In an English country garden.
Oh no, you really mustn't be seen, while we're being rude and mean,
In an English country garden."

They chortled at the end of their silly song. Walking into the front room once more, they were greeted by a ghastly sight.

Granddad Sprinkle-Tinkle gulped down the last drop of tea and ran the palm of one hand across his face. A long green streak squelched from his nose. He waxed it between both hands and ran the slimy streak through his hair.

"Gross," whispered Frances to Mary.

Whispering back, Mary shuddered, "Makes me feel sick."

As though Granddad Sprinkle-Tinkle had eyes in the back of his head, he sneered at them. "What are you two looking at? Haven't you ever seen a fine figure of a man before? And, I might add, a very handsome one at that."

"Sorry," apologised his granddaughter. "I was wondering where we should sit?"

"On your backside," snapped the old man, massaging his scalp. "Over there at the table."

Obediently doing as they were told, both girls started to colour some pictures.

"What do you think will happen when the Slug Busters start working?" whispered Mary, ever so quietly.

"When the gases get too much to hold in," Frances answered, "maybe his stomach will swell up."

"Then what?"

"When they finally start to escape, he might be sent flying around the room."

"Like a deflating balloon?"

"I hope so," smiled Frances Fidget-Knickers.

After they had coloured in three pictures each, they began to doubt the ability of the concoction.

Feelings of puzzlement fizzled away inside Frances, and she said, "I don't understand why it's not working! Surely it should have worked by now? My sums were right!"

"Maybe there's something you missed?"

Frances mumbled through her sums again. "One hundred and twenty ... divided by eight ... fifteen minutes ... spot on."

"Perhaps it doesn't work that way?"

"Oops," she gulped, realising her mistake.

"What's up?"

"It's not the quantity we give him that matters," her friend muttered. "It's the amount of time it takes to get into the bloodstream."

"Frances, you're starting to freak me out."

"The absorption rate doesn't change."

"The what?"

"The time it takes to start working."

"Well, it's been over two hours already?"

"I know. It's doing my head in just thinking about it," replied Frances softly.

"Maybe he's immune to Slug Busters?" suggested Mary, glancing over to where Granddad Sprinkle-Tinkle was sitting.

"How long has it been now exactly?"

Mary, with one eye still on Granddad Sprinkle-Tinkle and the other on her watch, gave the answer. "Two and a half hours."

"It would be just our luck that he's resistant to them," frowned Frances, disappointedly.

"Hold your horses," exclaimed Mary. "Take a look at that!"

Both of them turned. Both of them watched. Both of them, with faces twinkling with pleasure, gazed on in fascination.

With the weirdest looking expression on his face, Granddad Sprinkle-Tinkle's eyes began to squint in discomfort. Deep down in the pit of the old man's guts, the first beginnings of a violent storm were beginning to swirl around. The peculiar look was getting worse with every passing second, as the storm picked up speed.

The Slug Busters were now starting to do their work.

Slowly at first, Granddad Sprinkle-Tinkle's horrid face began to swell. It changed colour, from red to dark red, and it went on changing, from dark red to dark purple. With accompanying shrieks, tremendous eruptions began to explode.

In shades of excruciating pain, he cried out, "AAAGH! Me guts are on fire!"

Jumping to her feet and pretending to be surprised, Frances gasped. "Oh Granddad, you scared the life out of me! Goodness, you look ill!"

"Of course I am!" he yelped. "So would you be if you had this blimmin' guts-ache to put up with!"

"Blimey, you don't look too good," commented Mary.

A brilliant, stinging pain flashed inside the old man's guts, and he cried out again. "Oh, me old shoes and slippers! Even the taste of kippers is better than these pains in me innards! And you know how I hate kippers!"

Frances Fidget-Knickers' brain blew a thought. "Should I get you something? Anything? Maybe some medicine would help?"

"No way!" wheezed Granddad Sprinkle-Tinkle.

The next question was a master stroke of ingenuity.

"Perhaps I should call out the doctor?"

"Don't you dare!" cried the moth-eaten old man, whose pain-ridden face was erupting with sweat.

"But he could help you, Granddad."

"I don't want any medicine!"

"He's very good at getting people better."

"You know how I hate doctors! All they ever do is poke you and shovel a load of disgusting syrup down your throat!"

"But Doctor Light-Fingers isn't like that."

"I'm not having that thief over here!"

"Are you sure?" asked Frances, secretly admiring her trick.

"Do I have to say everything—" snapped Granddad Sprinkle-Tinkle, stopping short as the pain took over.

Frances Fidget-Knickers and Mary Midget-Mouth watched on.

"Oh no!" gasped her suffering grandfather.

Then he squinted in pain.

After that, he screwed his face up.

And then it happened, for the pain deep down was about to take over.

Aided by the toxic gases escaping, he stood to his feet and gasped some more. "I think I've got a bum-squidger coming!"

At lightning speed, with bum-thrusters gushing, he shot across the front room. With bottom-pumping puffs, he hurtled down the hallway. Now, with backside-thrusters firing at full pelt, he rocketed up the stairs to the only toilet in the house.

All the time this was going on, Frances and Mary were just two steps behind, making doubly sure not to be caught by the escaping bottom burps.

In his panic, Granddad Sprinkle-Tinkle grabbed the handle, the very handle that Frances had sabotaged earlier, and gave it a yank. Off it came, screws flying in every direction.

He looked on in disbelief.

"AAAGH!" cried the old man.

"Granddad, you must be stronger than you look!" exclaimed Frances, diverting his attention.

Waving the handle in the air and looking like he was going to explode, he shouted, "I used to do a bit of tug-of-war when I was young! Now all I want to do is pull down me trousers, because me guts are killing me!"

"Tug-of-war – really? I never knew that, Granddad."

Patting his behind with his free hand, he continued with the shouting. "I need to go to the toilet! I've got a pant-pusher trying to poke its way out!"

Cutting through the cries, Frances suggested, "Tell you what, Granddad, I'll go and get one of Daddy's screwdrivers."

"Good idea!" he spluttered. "Don't be all day about it. I don't know how much longer I can hold it in."

A little slower than the slowest snail, Frances Fidget-Knickers and Mary Midget-Mouth made their way to the kitchen. Once inside the great white room, they did not bother to go to the garage to fetch the screwdriver – because, all along, it sat hidden in Frances Fidget-Knickers' pocket.

Frances began to count even slower than the slowest snail, all the way up to one hundred.

Upstairs, the two girls heard Granddad Sprinkle-Tinkle coughing and spluttering. "Gawd blimey! Gawd help us! Gordon Bennett! I just don't know me own strength!"

Downstairs, the two girls smiled.

Upstairs, Granddad Sprinkle-Tinkle screamed out, "Gawd help us! Oh no! It's poking! I think I'm going to do it in me undies!"

Downstairs, Frances and Mary's smiles stretched to their fullest.

Upstairs, the commotion continued. "Crumbs, I'm going to have a blowout any minute now!"

Downstairs, Frances Fidget-Knickers punched the air. "Yes!" she cried.

"What a cracker!" beamed Mary, enthusiastically.

Again, upstairs desperate screams vibrated through the air and bounced off every wall in the house. "Oh my God, it's rush hour traffic up here! Where the hell are you, girly?"

Downstairs, Frances opened and closed the back door, making sure to bang it loudly.

Granddad Sprinkle-Tinkle's ears pricked up with the sudden noise. "That better be you, Frances!"

Counting quietly, she said mischievously, "One, two, miss a few, ninety-nine, one hundred."

With venom, the old man shouted out, "You better have a screwdriver, or there will be punishments!"

A gigantic lie washed over his granddaughters' lips as she shouted back, "I couldn't find a screwdriver at first, but I've got one now!"

Mary's mouth fell open mockingly. "Frances Fidget-Knickers, that's a whopper if ever I heard one! In fact, it's probably the most humungous piece of fibbing ever."

"Come on, let's see how he is," she laughed, dragging Mary from the kitchen.

When they reached the top of the stairs, they saw a curious sight. Granddad Sprinkle-Tinkle was on all fours, pounding the carpet with his fist.

"Me guts! Me guts! Me guts!" he cried, over and over again.

"Here you are, Granddad," smiled Frances, trying to hand over the screwdriver.

The old man stopped with the fist pounding and moaned through gritted teeth, "You're lucky – lucky, that is, that I'm not in a fit enough state to punish you!"

"I couldn't find it at first," fibbed Frances.

"The problem with children of today," insisted her grandfather, grinding his teeth, "is that they don't know what's good for them."

"It was behind the lawnmower."

"In my day, girly," steamed the old man, "kids got a good stiff whacking, just so their parents could have some fun."

"You can take it now, Granddad."

"By Christ," he puffed, "for not being quick enough, you would've had your backside whacked for sure."

To try and defuse the situation, Frances just said, "Sorry."

There was no time to carry on with his wicked ways. Hurriedly, the moaning old mongrel snatched the screwdriver. With trembling fingers, he tried to re-screw the tiny screws. Fumbling awkwardly, they slipped.

"Oh no, oh no, oh no," he gabbled, over and over again. "Get in there!"

"Do you need some help?" asked Frances.

"If I want your help, I'll ask for it!" barked Granddad Sprinkle-Tinkle. "Now, shut your mouth and let me get on with fixing this ruddy door handle!"

Mary stood back.

Inside the old man's guts, the venom of the mixing potion was beginning to become uncontrollable.

Puff, pump, whizz went the farts.

Frances joined Mary, as they stepped out of the way.

With stomach-crunching lightning flashes of thundering proportions, Granddad Sprinkle-Tinkle screamed almost insanely. "Come on! Do up! It's going to shoot out any second! Oh, me guts! Oh, me innards! I'm losing control of me bum-squidgers!"

Fascinated, Frances Fidget-Knickers and Mary Midget-Mouth watched on.

By now, Granddad Sprinkle-Tinkle was wheezing through clenched teeth.

Whizz, pop, pop, pop, whizz went the farts, as the first screw went in.

Inside the old man's guts more explosions happen.

Pop, pop, pop, whizz, pop went the bottom burps, as the second screw went in.

The explosions keep coming.

Crackle, pop, pop, squish, pop went the pant-wetting ones, as the third screw went in.

And the last explosions were the worst of all.

Bang, boom, thunder went the trumpeting farts, as the last screw was fixed into place.

Faster than a speeding cheetah, Granddad Sprinkle-Tinkle pulled open the door and dashed inside, slamming the door behind him.

Then they heard cries of panic.

"Blast! Me zip's stuck now! Keep calm! Come on! Get a grip! Blinking undo, won't you!"

A loud zipping noise sounded out as the zip loosened. "Haha, got you!"

Outside the toilet, Frances smiled. "That was a bit of a bonus!"

"Is the trick better than you'd hoped for?" asked Mary.

"Absolutely – the rotten old troll deserves it."

"That's really nasty."

"Pardon?"

"How could you insult a troll in such a way?" gasped Mary, teasingly. "A troll, next to the mean, unkind misfit behind this door, is a beautiful, elegant and noble creature."

Playfully making fun, Frances replied, "I do humbly apologise for my mistake in such matters concerning trolls."

"Apology accepted," Mary laughed.

From behind the toilet door, Granddad Sprinkle Tinkle interrupted their celebrations. Some very rude and disgusting noises were forcing their way through the air.

He gasped.

He grunted.

And then they heard the choking sounds of excruciating tummy pains come whooshing out.

Plop, *splatter*, and *splash* went the whooshers.

"ARGHHHH! OUCH OUCH! Ughhhhh!" sighed Granddad Sprinkle-Tinkle.

"Yuck!" shuddered Frances.

For a brief moment, all was still. Then the brief moment was shattered – as another lot of poop came gushing out.

"AHHHHH! That feels better!"

When the plopping and dolloping had finished, and after the toilet had been torpedoed several more times, a nasty smell of diarrhoea hit the air.

"Quick!" cried Frances. "Run for your life, it's a stink bomb!"

Delighted, Mary chased after Frances and stopped when they had finally reached the front room.

A little out of breath, Mary gasped, "Plan number one worked wonderfully well."

With a wolfish grin, Frances Fidget-Knickers agreed. "Revenge – it can be deliciously sweet."

"What's next?" asked Mary.

"There are magical feelings in these fingers, and you will have to wait and see …"

CHAPTER 6

THE FLAMING CONCOCTION

The morning had suddenly brightened up. There was a definite sense of victory as Frances and Mary moved to the large white kitchen.

The cottage shook.

Frances smiled at the ceiling and giggled, "House, did you enjoy that trick?"

Sure enough, House replied with a shudder, "YES!"

"Sorry, House, we can't stand around here all day," said Frances, excusing herself. "We've got to get on with the next one."

The cottage shook. "LET ME HELP YOU!" Wham, the kitchen blinds covering the window shot up, and a ray of sunlight stretched into the kitchen. "GOOD LUCK!"

"Thank you, House," she smiled gratefully.

"If I didn't know better," hushed Mary, slightly startled, "I'd say this cottage was haunted."

Pointing to the opposite side of the kitchen, a request for assistance came back. "I'm going to need some help."

Following the pointed arm, Mary asked, "Like what?"

"I'll need you to search for one small cooking pot and an icing bag."

"Are we making a cake?"

"The thinnest nozzle you can find."

"We're making a cake?"

"The wooden spoon and a large plastic syringe will be in the drawer over there."

"What kind of cake are we going to make?"

"When you've found them all, bring them over to me."

55

While Mary was searching, Frances began her task. "No, not there," she said, shutting one cupboard and opening the next. "I don't see them in here," Frances mumbled, shutting the second cupboard and opening the third. "There you are," she smiled eagerly, "and you four little darlings are coming with me, for we have much work to do."

Mary darted back over to her friend. Putting the items down, she asked, "Is this what you meant?"

"Perfect," answered Frances delightedly, after inspecting them all.

"So, what cake are we making then?"

"We're not making any cakes."

Gazing at the four containers sitting innocently on the work surface, Mary asked. "What are those then?"

Frances Fidget-Knickers began answering Mary's question by telling her about the ingredients. Pointing at each one individually, she said, "This one is Flame Throwing Powder. That one is Mouth Stinging Paste. These two are Tears of Pain Powder Very Hot, and Dragon's Breath of Fire Extra Hot."

Mary turned her nose up in disgust. "Who would be daft enough to eat that?"

"My father," laughed Frances.

"That's about right."

"I know all about these," smiled Frances. "My father loves his food incredibly hot. That's why we keep these mouth-burning things in the kitchen."

"He's nuts!"

"I couldn't agree more," Frances replied, and then she pretended to be her father. "Great Scott, it's wonderfully hot!"

Mary found this very funny. Frances went on with her mimicking. "By Heavens, I think this one is going to burn my bot!"

Great belly waves of laughter hit her friend, and she doubled over in stitches. "Stop, stop, stop!" she cried uncontrollably.

Still in Mr Rupert Flicker-Knickers mode, Frances went on, "The hotter the better, my old stinky sweater!"

Holding her stomach, Mary just couldn't say anything, for the fit of laughter had completely taken over.

"Pull yourself together," giggled Frances, changing her voice back to normal. "We've got work to do."

It was a few minutes before Mary Midget-Mouth had regained some sort of control over herself. In that time, a jug was found and filled with water.

"Are we going to cook something? If so, will we poison him?"

"No, we can't poison him," insisted Frances. "I'd like to, but we would become criminals."

"Would we?"

"Yes, and criminals always get caught and arrested."

"What would happen to us?"

"We would end up in court before a judge. After collecting the evidence, we would be sentenced to a stay at one of Her Majesty's prisons for a very long time."

"How long is a long time?"

"Until we were old and past it … or even longer."

"You can scrap that idea then."

Holding the jars up one at a time, Frances carried on. "These will do the job. It's legal … at least, I think it is."

Mary sniffed. "The smell – it's a dead give-away. He's going to know we've been cooking."

"Are we not young ladies," insisted Frances Fidget-Knickers, "with superior intelligence?"

"You're sounding like my mum."

"… who have the brainpower of a million, trillion Einsteins?"

"Perhaps not."

"… whereby we should easily manage to cover up the evidence?"

"Do you have a plan of action in mind?"

"While I'm mixing the ingredients in this saucepan, you will have to find the old tube of toothpaste upstairs."

Mary started on her checklist. "Check," she began.

"Which I think is in my mother's bedroom."

"Check."

"And you will need to bring it here."

"Check."

"You will also need to squeeze out the old tube, ready for refilling."

"Check."

"Saving a small amount."

"Check."

"Then I will refill it."

"Check."

"And you will return it from where it came."

"Check."

"Most important of all, you will need to run around the house spraying the air-freshener."

"Check, check and double check," beamed Mary, finishing her list with a question. "Why air-freshener?"

"To cover up the smell coming from the mixture," answered Frances, turning on the cooker and tipping the water into the saucepan.

"You're good," smiled Mary.

Placing the saucepan over the brightly coloured gas flame, Frances said cautiously, "The most important thing is to cover up this smell. In that way, we can palm it off on my grandfather's extremely bad wind."

"I see," she said, watching the Flame Throwing Powder dissolve into the water. "So he won't suspect anything."

"Got it in one," Frances replied, squeezing out the Mouth Stinging Paste. "Right, where's the teaspoon? I don't want to get the other ones on my hands, just in case I forget to wash them and rub some on my face."

"Those powders look harmless enough," Mary uttered, innocently.

"Don't let yourself be deceived," she blinked, spooning out some Tears of Pain powder. "Stings like hell if you get it in your eyes."

"It smells awful," sniffed Mary, as the Dragons Breath of Fire was added.

Now mixing the concoction, it thickened and turned dark red in colour. Lifting a dollop out of the saucepan it refused to drop off, and Frances said ecstatically, "Devil's juice!"

Mary shuddered with a gasp. "Don't like the look of that!"

"Keep your voice down," hushed Frances.

"Sorry, but it does look like it's glistening with evil spirits, and it smells terrible."

"Right, you know what to do."

When Mary had finished fetching the toothpaste and emptying it, saving a small amount on a spoon, she said in a military fashion, "Mission almost accomplished." Standing to attention, she saluted at the very end of her next sentence. "Just waiting for you to finish, then I will get on with spraying the air-freshener, Sir."

Frances, who wasn't quite listening, was concentrating very hard on the job at hand. "Got to get this right," she muttered, with the icing bag already filled.

With the thinnest of metal icing nozzles in place, she slowly began to squeeze out the demonised paste into the deflated tube. "Don't want any spillages."

The tube inflated until it looked almost normal again. As it did so, Mary's puzzling question came out. "Why do you need that small bit of toothpaste?"

"It's for the top of the tube. It will cover up the smell of the concoction," explained Frances, screwing on the cap.

"Clever idea," winked Mary.

"Action stations," beamed Frances Fidget-Knickers, handing over the tube.

"Fingers crossed, and wish me luck," said Mary Midget-Mouth.

"Luck has nothing to do with it," smiled Frances. "We are professionals – and don't forget the air-freshener."

Mary scuttled to the foot of the stairs and bounded two by two to the top, suddenly realising she was making too much noise and stopping.

"Gordon Bennett!" cried out Granddad Sprinkle-Tinkle.

It was a shout so loud that she nearly hit the roof. With the tube of flaming toothpaste in one hand and the air-freshener in the other, her brain reminded her with a heart-thumping breathlessness to creep quietly.

Granddad Sprinkle-Tinkle cried out again. "Won't it ever stop?"

Quickly realising that she had not been caught, Mary Midget-Mouth replaced the tube and swiftly returned to the kitchen, after spraying the air-freshener everywhere.

"How'd it go?" asked Frances, putting the cake-making equipment away.

"I thought we were in for it," sighed Mary. "He only went and shouted out as I was creeping past the toilet."

"I heard," smiled Frances, folding up the tea towel. "He won't be saying much after this trick!"

"Now that'd be music to my ears," exhaled Mary.

"That it might be," said Frances, thinking hard. "Let's not get sloppy. We need to check that everything we've used is back in its right place."

"Will he notice?"

Checking through the cupboards, Frances Fidget-Knickers inspected them all. "If there is one thing out of place, he will know it. Then we'll be found out, and you know what that means?"

"Punishments."

"You got it in one."

Eventually, the toilet door opened and, in between gasps, Granddad Sprinkle-Tinkle called out, "Frances! Mary! I want you both here, at once!"

"Coming!" shouted both girls.

It happened the minute they both reached the top of the landing. Granddad Sprinkle-Tinkle looked at them with distrust. "What did you put in me drink?"

"Now ... let me see," thought Frances.

"Being careful, are we?" asked the horrid old man, suspiciously eyeing both of them. "Got something to hide, have we?"

"No, of course not," insisted his granddaughter.

"Well, what was it? Did you spike me drink? Wouldn't put it past your friend standing there," he said, grouchily.

With one hand held behind her back, Frances crossed her fingers. "Definitely not. Mary and I, we would never do such a thing."

He hissed a hideous hiss, and grumble, "Something is wrong – I can smell it!"

Convincingly, his granddaughter stretched the truth. "We put milk in, a teabag, the hot water then the ten sugars, just like you asked."

The wicked old man glared at them. "All ten?" he asked.

Frances stopped and faced Mary. "Mary counted them to make sure we got it right. Didn't you, Mary?"

She nodded in agreement.

Granddad Sprinkle-Tinkle blasted at Mary, "Counted? Show me!"

This was not a time to be slow. Now was a time to react quickly. So Mary counted to ten very fast and, at the end, she said, "See? Not one mistake."

"Blasted dingbats!" fumed the old man.

Diplomatically, this was now a time for both girls to remain silent.

With no ammunition left to fire at them, he fumed some more. "It's your mother's fault! Got to be the shopping! Changes cause nothing but trouble! Changes don't agree with me one bit! It's changes that's given me this ruddy guts-ache! And I definitely know it's something to do with that new sugar which has given me this runny undercarriage!"

"Do you think so?" asked Frances.

"What's up with you?" sniffed her horrible grandfather, sticking his nose in the air snootily. "It's plainer than the nose on your face. Your mother, plus the wrong sugar, equals me guts-ache. Can't be any simpler than that, now, can it?"

"I would never have thought of that," chipped in Mary. "Would you, Frances?"

"No, not in a month of Sundays," agreed Frances, shaking her head.

"Twits!" snapped Granddad Sprinkle-Tinkle, still snootily displaying his nose. "If rotting meat was wit, then both your heads would be full of it!"

The putrid smell wafting from the toilet assaulted Frances Fidget-Knickers' nose as she asked, "Granddad, do you feel better now?"

"Of course I don't feel better!" he snapped again. "The best bit of me has gone down the toilet! That experience in there has left a nasty taste in me mouth!"

"What about brushing your teeth? You know, to get rid of the taste," suggested Frances cunningly.

"Not sure about that. Don't want to ruin them. Taken years to get them looking this good," insisted Granddad Sprinkle-Tinkle, thoughtfully.

"Don't then," she huffed, folding her arms.

Mary shot Frances an awkward glance, as if to say "but that's what we want him to do".

"You'll just have to put up with the taste," continued Frances, keeping her arms folded and shrugging them carelessly.

He wheezed. "You'd like that, wouldn't you? You'd like to see your poor old Granddad suffer! But I'm not going to give you the pleasure. So I've decided that, just this once, I will give them a brush."

"You'll feel much better afterwards," she smiled, unfolding her arms.

The old man coughed. "Seeing as I haven't got a toothbrush of me own, I'm going to use yours."

This caught Frances by surprise. "Okay then," she gasped.

Granddad Sprinkle-Tinkle tucked in his clothes and forced his way past Frances and Mary, naturally dismissing them as he did so.

From behind, the two girls watched him tugging at his shirt. With an unspoken agreement, they held hands.

"Which one's yours?" snorted Granddad Sprinkle-Tinkle, entering the bathroom.

"My toothbrush is the green one," answered Frances.

"Where's the toothpaste gone?" he grumbled, not seeing it anywhere.

"In Mummy's room," answered Frances.

"Well, get it for me."

So she did, and she gave it to her very nasty grandfather.

"Get lost, you two," grumbled Granddad Sprinkle-Tinkle, snatching the tube of toothpaste. "I don't want any interfering little brats watching."

Unscrewing it, he sniffed. "Hold up a minute."

They both froze in fear.

He paused to sniff the air some more. "What's that I can smell? What have you two been playing at?"

Alarm bells rang. Mary's legs went unbelievably weak, but she managed to force herself to stand.

Swallowing hard, Frances showed no sign of being panicked, asking in a steady and level voice, "What smell, Granddad?"

"You've both been messing around. Don't you be denying it," sniffed Granddad Sprinkle-Tinkle again.

"We haven't," insisted Frances, with unblinking eyes.

With a hint of punishments yet to come, he sniffed some more. "You've both been using perfume – haven't you?" He sniffed even more deeply and smiled nastily. "And you don't have any perfume, do you?"

"No, I don't," agreed Frances. "We used the air-freshener."

Still sniffing the air, he snapped in disappointment, "What for?"

65

"To cover up that terrible smell coming from the toilet," Frances replied.

Her horrid grandfather fumed in disappointment. "I ought to knock your block off! You're both as useless as a lead balloon!"

Frances and Mary held their breath, for the smell really was awful.

"Nature!" the old man blasted out. "That's what you smelt! And I suppose yours doesn't stink?"

In fear of an even nastier tongue lashing if they answered back, they both remained silent.

"You two can stay where you are. That way, you can't get up to anything," seethed Granddad Sprinkle-Tinkle.

"That's fine by us," said Frances, swinging Mary's arm.

Reluctantly, he squeezed the toothpaste out onto the green toothbrush. It came snaking out and over the bristles. On top, a large red body with a white head sat ready for a serpent's strike. The parting between his lips grew wider as the toothbrush disappeared. Swallowing uneasily, he began to ram the brush from side to side.

"Not too bad," mumbled the rotten old worm, reassuring himself. "Mind you, it's a little warm."

"Toothpaste can be warm – even hot, if you've put too much on the brush," said Frances Fidget-Knickers.

"Can it?" he mumbled.

Now the chance had come to tell the nastiest grandfather in the world something that was sure to warm things up – for, on the Dragon's Breath of Fire Extra Hot container, it advised "reacts violently with water".

Casually, Frances suggested, "Maybe you need to rinse your mouth out."

"Even idiots can have a good idea," he sniffed, bending down to sip some water.

66

The water did nothing to stop the flaming concoction. In fact, it had the opposite effect. Steadily, it began to heat up.

It went from cool to warm.

Then it went from warm to hot.

Finally, it ignited with the heat of a fire-breathing dragon bellowing out its flames. Bursting into a towering inferno, Granddad Sprinkle-Tinkle spluttered, "AAAGH! Holy smoke! Me gob's alight!"

Frances cried out, "Granddad, you've gone all funny-looking again!"

Clutching both hands around his throat and flicking his tongue in and out like a snake, he shrieked, "Me mouth's on fire!"

The snaking tongue was watched with great joy.

"Ow-w-w! It feels like me throat's being ripped out from the inside!" he screamed. "I knew it! I knew me mouth was too sensitive for that toothpaste! I can't keep drinking water all day! I'll end up looking like a beer barrel! Whatever will I do?"

"Granddad, you need something more powerful than water – it might be a germ."

"Eureka!" cried Granddad Sprinkle-Tinkle. "I think you're onto something!" Picking up a yellow plastic bottle, he tore off the top and spoke just before guzzling down the liquid. "I'm going to disinfect me mouth!"

Before he started to guzzle, Frances said. "I don't think I like the sound of that, Granddad, it might not taste too—"

"Never mind that, girl," he snapped, cutting her short.

"But—" Frances tried to speak again.

Granddad Sprinkle-Tinkle let out an ear-piercing shriek. "AAAGH! Me gob's hotter than a grill! AAAGH! You could cook steak in there! In two seconds flat it would come out well done!"

Tipping the bottle, he took one enormous gulp. Instantly, the liquid sprayed from his lips. "Yuck! That's disgusting!" he spluttered. Then he coughed out, "If something's not done in a hurry then I'm going to go completely off me trolley!"

Concealing her admiration for the effects of the liquid, Frances asked, "Is it still painful, Granddad?"

"What do you think?" yelped Granddad Sprinkle-Tinkle, slightly bewildered.

Mary added to the state of confusion. "Whatever will you do?"

"Do?" he screamed. "Do?" he gasped. "How should I know? AAAGH! Someone grab a fire extinguisher!"

"Have we got a fire extinguisher?" asked Frances Fidget-Knickers.

"I don't think we have!" screamed her grandfather.

"I think you're right," agreed Frances.

With tears, he cried, "Call out the fire brigade instead!"

"We can't do that, Granddad," insisted Frances.

"Why not?" cried the old man. "It's a simple request! All you have to do is ring them!"

Knowing that this was a naughty thing to do, Frances stated, "It would be a misuse of the emergency services. You can get fined a lot of money for that."

"Oh shut up, you know-it-all!" Granddad Sprinkle-Tinkle said sharply.

Just then, Mary came out with her suggestion. "It might be wise to eat something. You know, to take away the taste."

"Don't be an idiot!" bellowed the old man. "If I eat anything, I'll be upsetting me stomach again!"

"Oh!" gulped Mary.

"Is that all you've got to say for yourself?" boomed Granddad Sprinkle-Tinkle.

"No," said Mary, faltering. Realising her mistake, she quickly spluttered, "I mean yes!"

The smell of rotten eggs came hurtling towards Mary Midget-Mouth as Granddad Sprinkle-Tinkle shouted across the bathroom, "When you grow up, you'll be just like your father!"

"Really?" Mary said, very proudly.

"A dimwit!" cried the old man.

"Oh," gasped Mary, her mouth wide open in shock.

With all the shouting and spluttering, plus the coughing and choking, the worst grandfather you could possibly imagine had sprayed his clothes with spit, which contained the flaming toothpaste.

"Granddad," Frances said softly. "I think your clothes need washing."

Eyeing them in the mirror, Granddad Sprinkle-Tinkle thundered, "Blast it! Look at me Sunday best!" Wheeling around towards his granddaughter, he glared with utter disgust and fumed, "It's all over me! Your fault – and don't argue back!"

Brushing his clothes, he calmed himself a little. "You can wash them." Wetting a flannel, he finally shut up, but not before he moaned one last time. "I'll be in me bedroom getting undressed. I'll shout, when I want them back."

With that, the unexpected opportunity had opened up, as Frances informed him, "You won't get them back today, Granddad. By the time I've washed and dried them, it will be tomorrow morning."

"Useless," he muttered, with the flannel stuck inside his mouth, then he disappeared into his bedroom.

Frances waited for the door to shut. Now with the set of circumstances that enable things to happen, she smiled, "That's just given me an idea. We need to see Godfrey."

CHAPTER 7

GODFREY

The bathroom was a mess. Spit stains ran down the mirror. The empty bottle of disinfectant lay in the bath, and the tube of toothpaste was left in the sink.

"You said not to leave anything that might give the game away," stressed Mary. "What about the toothpaste?"

"I've not forgotten," answered Frances Fidget-Knickers, anxiously. "But we need to check he's not going to come out."

Mary waited for the signal.

Frances pricked up her ears – they had become even more efficient than before – and leant against her grandfather's bedroom door. "Right, you get the toothpaste and I will listen out for any signs of trouble."

Inside Granddad Sprinkle-Tinkle's room, Frances heard him moaning. "Me best clothes! Look at them! I hate clean clothes. Don't smell right after they've been washed. Never feel the same either."

"Got it," Mary smiled, showing her the tube.

"Hide it," Frances said quickly.

The door to Granddad Sprinkle-Tinkle's bedroom opened and out popped his head, and only his head. "Take them," he insisted, handing over the clothes.

"Okay," cringed Frances, holding the stinky garments.

"If I was half-decent," moaned the old man, "I'd come out there and show you both the back of me hand."

Mary looked at Frances awkwardly. Frances looked back and shushed with her lips.

Eyes now twinkling menacingly, Granddad Sprinkle-Tinkle slammed the door. From behind it, he shouted, "No disturbances while I'm reading up on me oriental torturing book! I might consider putting bamboo shoots under your fingernails later!"

"Does he mean it?" winced Mary.

"Maybe, you never know. He might have a change of heart, but then we would be asking for a miracle," she laughed, not really caring.

"A heart – I didn't know he had one," said Mary, incredulously.

Shouting at the closed door, Frances asked, "When I've washed them, Granddad, can we go down to the cellar?"

"Do what you want! Leave me alone! I'm reading!" sulked Granddad Sprinkle-Tinkle.

The room fell silent and off they went.

"Do we have to wash them?" sighed Mary, lethargically. "I bet when they're clean I'll be the one running up these stairs again."

Now halfway down the stairs her friend insisted, "A little exercise never killed anyone.

Mary huffed, "Really? What, never?"

"Sometimes small sacrifices have to be made," she answered, taking a few more steps.

"Never ever?" huffed Mary again.

Now at the bottom, Frances turned and held up the garments. "At least you are not holding these."

Grabbing her nose she gagged. "I might die if I was holding them. They must stink to high heaven!"

"You're not far wrong there," agreed Frances, wrinkling her face in disgust. "Should only take a couple of minutes to get this lot sorted out, and we can be on our way."

"We are lucky," began Mary, now watching Frances load up the washing machine. "Lucky it's not raining, that is."

"Can't stand around here all day," she smiled, switching the machine on. "Even if it rains here, it's not going to matter where we are going."

"Oh yes," said Mary excitedly.

With her excitement overflowing she palled at her friends clothes. "Come on Mary, we need to see Godfrey."

"What for?"

"For the next two tricks, I will need to go back to my world," smiled Frances Fidget-Knickers.

"I like the sound of that."

"You know the only time we are allowed in is when we are with Godfrey."

"Oh, I see – we cannot get them unless Godfrey is with us."

Approaching the cellar door Frances replied. "That's what I've been trying to say."

The entrance to the cellar was dark. Black iron holders fixed to the walls held naked flames that lit up the cobbled stairs. Patches of green moss dotted the way down. A curved metal handrail flowed on in front of them. It started to become cold and damp the further they went down the passageway.

They finally came to the end of the long, winding steps and into a large open space. The emptiness was dimly lit.

"I see that you have made it safely down the stairs," came a voice from the darkness. The voice was polite and well spoken.

"Please turn the lights up, Godfrey," said Frances, recognising who was speaking.

As the light lifted, the darkness was swallowed.

Godfrey sat behind a tall desk, and from what you could see, he was a rat.

73

A well-dressed rat.

The rodent was writing in a book.

"Do come closer," said Godfrey, scribbling away. "My eyes are not as young as they used to be."

Both of them walked forwards.

"Good afternoon, Miss Frances," smiled the rat, moving his attention away from the book in front of him.

"Hello Godfrey," she answered politely.

He wore a small monocle over his left eye, and it dropped out as he spoke, "Why, I do believe that is Miss Mary with you, Miss Frances." With that, he stopped writing and flicked some pages.

"Hello Godfrey," beamed Mary. "It's really nice to see you again."

"It is?" asked the rodent, stopping briefly and looking puzzled. "Did you not see me the last time we met?"

"Yes, and I was being polite."

"I certainly have lost weight," expressed Godfrey, mishearing Mary, his attention returning to the book. "I feel as light as a feather these days. Been working out, you know. By my records, it has been nearly three weeks since your last visit."

Godfrey came out from behind the desk, replaced his monocle and stood in front of them. He stood to about half the height of the two girls. What a dashing little fellow he was. He was wearing a three-piece pinstripe suit and a white shirt, topped off with a beautiful, chequered bow tie. Cane in hand, he walked towards them with highly polished shoes clipping.

Godfrey stopped some five paces away and chuckled, "House has been telling me about your tricks. We've been having quite a laugh about it. So, you want to go to Mrs Give-Us-A-Giggle's shop?"

"How did you know that? I've not told anyone."

"House is very old and very wise. House knows all there is to know about everything," smiled Godfrey. "I think that I could be of some assistance to you, Miss Frances."

"Does he?" asked Mary, referring to House.

"House is not a 'he'," informed Godfrey.

"Sorry," said Mary. "My mistake. Does she?"

"House is not a 'she', either," Godfrey answered.

"If House is not a he or a she, then what is it?" said Mary, confused.

"House is a cottage named House," answered Godfrey.

"Now I'm completely lost," sighed Mary, scratching her head.

"Would you like to know more?" he asked, waving them closer.

They didn't waste much time waiting for Godfrey to ask again, and moved five very fast steps forwards.

Now that all three were standing together, the rat said, "House has agreed to help."

Then he tapped the floor with his beautiful cane. Faster than it takes for a thought to even begin to become a thought, the ground opened up and they were falling down a chute.

"Cripes!" cried Frances Fidget-Knickers.

"Help!" screamed Mary Midget-Mouth.

"Whoopee! It's the only way to get there!" shouted the rodent.

Several more minutes of falling ended up with all three sliding into a large basket.

"We are here!" smiled Godfrey, picking himself up and dusting himself down. "Anyone got a light?"

"What for?" asked both girls, who were still brushing themselves off and had no idea where they were.

"So we can be on our way," he said, looking up.

Frances and Mary followed his eyes. Above them sat a frame, supporting a large metal burner. Above that, there was a quivering, billowing sheet of cloth.

"It's a balloon," gasped Frances in astonishment.

"That it is," replied Godfrey.

"I thought you said we were here?" asked Mary, somewhat puzzled.

"We are," answered Godfrey. "Now, where did I put that light?"

"Sorry, I'm not allowed matches."

"Nor me," said Mary.

"Not to worry," smiled Godfrey, dusting off his cane. "I'll just use this."

With a tap of the beautifully engraved cane, a spark jetted out and lit the burner. The balloon filled with hot air and started to lift. In the flicker of the flames, both girls looked around and saw what seemed to resemble the surface of the moon.

"Crikey!" Mary gasped, leaving her mouth open.

From inside the balloon, the ground moved outwards and upwards at a steep incline. All around were huge boulders, stained by the distant fires of hell. Jagged rocks with their razor edges gave off vivid images of death and destruction.

"Where are we?" asked Frances.

"We are inside a volcano," answered Godfrey. "Miss Frances and Miss Mary, please could you untie those sandbags."

"I hope it doesn't erupt while we're still in it," gulped Mary.

"I wouldn't worry too much about that," said Godfrey, helping with the sandbags. "It's extinct."

With less weight, the balloon rose higher and climbed free of the crater.

"So is this how we are getting to Mrs Give-Us-A-Giggle's shop?" asked Frances.

"Not without a permit," insisted Godfrey. "You cannot go walking around a world you have been banished from without asking for a Day Pass."

"Why not?" asked Mary.

"There are bounty hunters out there," shuddered Godfrey, loosening some more sandbags. "No matter how small you are, you would be considered fair game."

"But we've never had to ask for one before!" Frances protested.

With a knowledgeable smile, Godfrey answered. "You have never wanted to take anything back with you before."

Half-knowing the answer, Mary asked. "That would be House, I take it?"

"Correct!" beamed Godfrey proudly, with a sudden urgency to adjust some controls.

He pulled some levers.

Then he pushed them back into position.

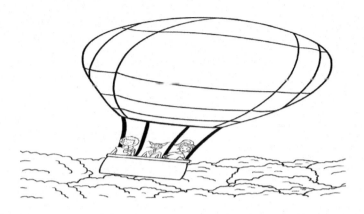

Not quite happy with what he had done, the leavers got pulled once more. Finally, when he was happy the rodent shut them off.

Now the balloon had climbed so high that the trees below looked like little sticks of broccoli. All three were looking down. Great valleys of green washed over the land. Tiny streams ran into large ones and became small rivers. Pockets of fields blossomed marvellously. Fantastic views sparkled over their eyes and continued for miles around.

The lemon sun was so warm and cosy that Mary let slip without even thinking. "It is so beautiful – who would ever want to leave this place?"

"I'm afraid Miss Frances did not get a say in the matter," declared Godfrey, pulling down a lever.

Suddenly, a jet of fire shot out, and the noise of a burning flame took over. Frances and Mary leant back, away from the heat.

The rigid bar was only held for a few seconds. "Sorry about that – we needed some more height. As I was saying, Frances was not at fault, it was Granddad Sprinkle-Tinkle."

"No surprise there," said Mary.

"Miss Mary, the Ministry of Justice found something they did not like."

"What did they find?" asked Frances Fidget-Knickers.

Godfrey shook his head and sighed. "Miss Frances, at first they suppressed it, ignored it, and swept it under the carpet. All that ever happens when you do that … it means the dirt is still there."

"What happened?" asked Mary.

"He only managed to wriggle out by paying them off and not giving evidence."

Frances gasped in shock. "How did he manage that?"

"Miss Frances, he had incriminating things on people. Nasty incriminating things they must have been."

"What things?" Mary asked.

"Things that would send people in high places to prison … so he never spoke out against them."

"Not one word?" gulped Frances, still a little shocked.

"Not one, Miss Frances, and that got him a reduced sentence, from death to banishment."

"Banishment?" puzzled Mary.

"And that included all the family," sighed Godfrey.

This was the first time that Mary had heard the story, because Frances never talked about such matters freely. Somehow, deep down inside, Mary felt feelings of compassion for her friend's grandfather. "Your poor Granddad!"

"Poor Granddad?" laughed Godfrey. "More like poop Granddad from what House has been saying! And House still thinks he's an old hook-nosed pig of the sea!"

An infectious bout of laughter took over while the balloon still carried on upwards and onwards.

"Old hook-nosed!" laughed Frances Fidget-Knickers.

"Pig!" coughed Mary Midget-Mouth.

"Of the sea!" spluttered Godfrey.

It was at this point that Frances decided to educate them. "Did you know that hook-nosed pigs of the sea are grey seals," she said, with a giggle. "Grey seals are pinnipeds, and pinniped is Latin for wing or fin-footed."

During their moment of learning and light laughter, the balloon had now climbed to its maximum height. A gentle breeze floated into the basket and calmed them down.

"That was a good one," sighed Godfrey. "If it was not for House, I'm not sure what your family would have done."

"What do you mean?" asked Frances, not knowing this part of her family's history.

"Now, let me see. You wouldn't, would you, know about such things as People Agents? You are far too young to know about such things," sniffed Godfrey, thoughtfully.

"People Agents?" asked Frances.

"Who are they?" asked Mary.

"Miss Frances and Miss Mary, in this world Houses decide who they want to live in them."

"Do they?" Frances said.

"Yes – they ask People Agents to find suitable people to live in them."

"I never would have thought of it," said Mary, rubbing her chin.

"After deciding which person they like, a solicitor is instructed to do the necessary paper work, and low and behold, it's a legally binding contract."

In her moment of despair, Frances sighed. "Why me? Why did I have to get stuck with the world's worst grandfather?"

"Miss Frances, being an upstanding and honourable cottage, House stayed faithful to the document it had signed."

Godfrey stopped to think. Frances and Mary stood and waited.

Smiling at them both, he continued, "In Mary's world, they might call their dwellings chalet, flats, bungalows and many more different names besides. In this world, no matter what their size and shape, they all answer to the same name."

"Blinking whatsits," gasped Mary Midget-Mouth. "That must cause a lot of confusion when they hold house meetings."

"You mean it was House that saved the family?" asked Frances Fidget-Knickers.

"Afraid so," replied Godfrey.

"I had no idea," smiled Frances, gratefully.

Mary gave her friend the biggest cuddle ever. "House must really, really like you."

With passion in her voice, Frances said, "Good old House. The next tricks are for you."

Godfrey frowned. Then he shook his head. "Not once in all this time has that despicable grandfather of yours thanked House. If it was not for House, you'd be homeless. That is why House has decided to help."

"He's out of order!" insisted Mary.

"Wish we could put a sign on him saying 'out of order'," frowned Frances, crossly.

"Oh, that's a good one, Miss Frances, but I have no time for laughing," puffed Godfrey, holding in a giggle. "We really should be getting ready to land."

During the next few minutes, Godfrey turned down the burner and the balloon gently fell. Trees, rivers and land became bigger again as they talked more.

"So what did he do then?" asked Frances, watching Godfrey going about his business.

"Sorry, Miss Frances, I have not got the time to explain at the moment," he said, peering over the basket.

To peer over the basket, Godfrey was standing on the tips of his toes, his nose twitching frantically. "Got to get this right – we don't want a crash landing."

The ground below was getting nearer and nearer. They were now descending upon a city so gigantic, so magnificent and wondrous, that all Frances and Mary could do was watch in amazement.

"My hometown," smiled the rodent, turning the valve down a little more. "Quite extraordinary, don't you think?"

Still they looked down in amazement as rows and rows of houses wobbled and quivered. Great chimneys puffed out whipped-cream clouds. Even though it was daytime, liquorice lampposts shone with their lemon-sherbet flames. Raspberry-red postboxes glistened deliciously, while chocolate-covered paths flowed into toffee-covered roads. People below them, unlike anyone they had ever seen, pointed at the balloon coming in to land.

They were now within spitting distance of the ground, and Godfrey cried out excitedly, "The city of Confectionery, here we come!"

The landing was soft, and not one person on the ground got squashed. Godfrey, Frances and Mary watched as a large crowd of odd-looking people gathered around.

They all had different coloured heads.

And there were only three colours to be seen.

"Godfrey, why do they look like that?" asked Frances.

"I would like to know that, too!" chipped in Mary. "They look very strange!"

"Well," began Godfrey, pointing his cane, "as you can see, Miss Frances and Miss Mary, here we have the Black Heads. There are the Yellow Heads. And over there are the White Heads. They all belong to the bacteria family."

"You mean they're spots?" asked Mary.

"My dear child, of course they are spots – it comes from having a very bad diet and not washing," insisted Godfrey.

The next moment, before either one of the two girls could respond, a shout from behind the crowd boomed out.

"Come on, out of the way! Make way for the Justice of the Peace!"

Like the parting of the sea, the crowd opened. A fat figure of a man walked through the opening. With short, stubby arms and legs, he shuffled along, blowing like a pig.

Coming to a stop, he demanded, "And who said you could land this contraption here?"

"Judge Get-It-Wrong," answered Godfrey.

"Did he?" huffed the fat man.

"Yes," said Godfrey. "What's more, we have the document right here, giving us the permission to do so."

The fat man took the important-looking bit of paper and began to read. "By order of the Supreme Court, I, Judge Get-It-Wrong, give permission for Godfrey and two companions to land in the city of Confectionery."

The fat man shoved the document back towards Godfrey and said, "Highly irregular. Follow me."

"Where are we going?" asked Frances and Mary.

"To court!" answered the fat man.

CHAPTER 8

THE COURTROOM

After several minutes of following the fat man, everything changed into winter. It was now very cold. There was now snow on the ground.

"Why on earth would you put a courtroom out here?" asked Frances Fidget-Knickers.

The fat man shuffled along, leaving footprints in the snow. "The legal process can be a very cold and frosty environment at times," he answered.

Great ice sheets the size of skyscrapers reached up into the sky and disappeared through the clouds.

The most beautiful building came into view across a polar region of frozen water. Brittle, transparent windows, longer and wider than an average sized car, covered almost two thirds of the structure. Underfoot, the frozen water cracked with each passing step.

"The ground is moving!" exclaimed Frances.

"Not to worry, Miss Frances, it's quite natural," Godfrey said, calmingly. "At the moment we are walking on top of a frozen lake, and every now and then the ice expands, making those cracking noises."

"Will it break?" asked Mary, jumping up and down.

"If you keep doing that," voiced the fat man, walking up some crystal steps, "I dare say it will."

Godfrey walked two paces behind the fat man, followed by the two girls.

"What is it?" Mary asked Frances, staring at the huge building.

Before her friend had a chance to answer, the fat man butted in. "It's the High Court of Justice." Then he added, still trotting up the steps, "Courthouse, in layman's terms."

"Blooming big house if you ask me," winked Frances to Mary.

"This," cried Godfrey, in a high-pitched voice aimed at drowning out Frances Fidget-Knickers' remark, "is where we get the permits from!"

They hurried up the icy-clear steps in silence and the enormous crystal door opened. Everything changed as they passed through it.

The floor was made from white marble with tiny, blue stress lines. Row after row of doors continued down a never-ending corridor. The passageway was empty.

As they walked along, Frances couldn't help herself. "Never thought I would be doing the ten thousand metres!"

"More like the marathon," winked Mary.

Godfrey looked over his shoulder and said, "Miss Frances and Miss Mary, we will have no tomfoolery in this place. It's an establishment of law and order. Serious things are discussed in this building and behind those doors. We do not want to jeopardise anything, now, do we?"

Both girls shook their heads.

The fat man nodded in agreement with Godfrey, while pointing to the sign attached to one of them. "The Court of Appeal, for people who find it hard to get a date. Worked for me – that's where I met the wife."

They quickly carried on, as room after room was passed.

Then, without warning, the chubby fellow pointed to another door. "The European Court of Human Rights," he said, with a shake of his hand. "There are no wrongs behind that door – or, come to think of it, no lefts either."

Still the little fat man carried on down the corridor, and still he talked on. "This one is the Queen's Bench Division. Not bad chairs, I can tell you."

Godfrey proudly agreed. "Very comfy indeed – I have a couple at home."

The tubby man's pace quickened, and with his head, he nodded and explained, "Behind there you have the Civil Court. Nothing ever gets done; they're all too polite."

"At least someone is nice," said Frances, thinking of her horrid grandfather.

Now pacing along at full marching speed, the roly-poly chap pointed. "Over there we have the Official Referees' Court. What a lot of whistle blowing, such a noise!"

They passed a door so small that not even a mouse could enter.

"Whatever could you use that room for?" asked Mary.

"Small claims," answered the fat man.

They were now walking up to the very last door. The sound of their shoes clipping against the marble seemed to take over as they stopped talking.

"Here we are," said the fat man, pushing the door open.

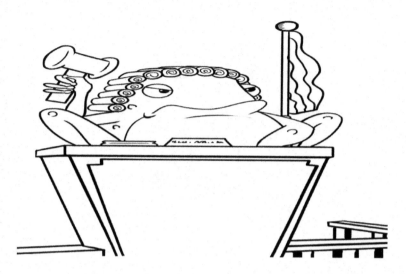

He entered the room, followed by Godfrey, Frances and Mary. The courtroom bustled with excitement. Seated in the public gallery and in every nook and cranny were odd-looking people, talking amongst themselves. To the far end and to the right, there were twelve individuals sitting in a jury box. To the left, the dock stood empty. In front of them, as they walked on, was the bench.

A bullfrog sat behind the bench, with a little wooden hammer in his hand. The other hand was trying to adjust a wig, which sat very oddly over his head, almost covering one eye.

"Hurry up! Move along!" cried the bullfrog. "We haven't got all day! I'll have no dilly-dallying in my court!"

"Right you are, Judge Get-It-Wrong," said the fat man, lengthening his stride.

Frances Fidget-Knickers and Mary Midget-Mouth were forced into the dock. The enclosure in the courtroom was small, so small that there was really only enough room for one person to stand comfortably, but still they were pushed inside.

Godfrey sat opposite them and said, "Good luck!"

"Good Heavens!" cried Judge Get-It-Wrong, staring at Frances and Mary. "What are they?"

"They're children," came a voice from the back of the court.

Everyone turned.

Everyone looked.

There, at the back of the courtroom, stood a tall insect of a figure, dressed in seventeenth century clothing. "To be precise, little girls."

"Ha, Mr Never-Won-A-Case!" cried Judge Get-It-Wrong. "Nasty looking things, aren't they?"

Mr Never-Won-A-Case made his way gracefully to the front of the court, with long lanky strides and asked, "Haven't you ever seen a child before, your Honour?"

"Not in my courtroom," huffed Judge Get-It-Wrong. "I don't do juvenile crime."

"No, you don't, your Honour," agreed Mr Never-Won-A-Case.

The judge rubbed his nose and asked, "I take it that you will be defending and prosecuting all at the same time?"

"Yes, your Honour," beamed the solicitor, flicking some dirt off his very grand clothes.

"Damned good show, saving us money like that!" cried Judge Get-It-Wrong, waving his hammer in the air.

Frances shouted over to both of them. "How can you defend someone and prosecute them all at the same time? You need two solicitors, don't you?"

The judge coughed and spluttered simultaneously and said to Frances, "Do you not know?"

"Know what?" she asked.

Focusing back on Mr Never-Won-A-Case, Judge Get-It-Wrong sniffed. "She doesn't know, you know. She didn't even address me correctly. You will have to explain, my dear chap."

"I'd be delighted to, your Honour," said the solicitor, turning to address Frances and Mary. "My dear clients, I'm a humble servant of the legal profession with split personalities. Inside this head of mine are two of the finest minds, fighting over good and evil."

"There you go, quite simple really," insisted the judge with a look of boredom.

Mr Never-Won-A-Case paused deep in thought, his antennae twitching, and stared into nothing.

"Who's ever heard of such a thing?" asked Mary, watching the solicitor.

Mr Never-Won-A-Case turned without answering and looked out over the courtroom. With arms opened wide, he declared, "It's absurd, even unthinkable, for two solicitors to be in this courtroom at any one time! Think of the wasted time, then think of the costs! One body, two minds, one cost! So, you see, I save this good city a fortune in legal fees!"

The courtroom filled with clapping hands of approval, as a Mexican wave of rising and falling bodies celebrated the speech.

"Why, thank you, how kind," bowed Mr Never-Won-A-Case.

After bowing, he spoke again to Frances and Mary. "When addressing Judge Get-It-Wrong, you must call him 'your Honour'."

"Oh brother, we're guilty," sighed Mary.

"Right!" cried Judge Get-It-Wrong, banging his small hammer. "Let's get on with the job at hand! Court is now in session!"

The courtroom fell silent.

"Your Honour," began Mr Never-Won-A-Case, "the reason for my clients being here is because they would like a Day Pass."

"Really, are they any good?" asked Judge Get-It-Wrong, leaning forwards. "Blasted tricky manoeuvre, that Day Pass."

"Forgive me, your Honour; I'm a little lost on this line of questioning?"

"Football," smiled the judge. "We could do with a couple of new members in our team. There's nothing like a bit of young blood to get things moving. Mind you, they do look a little bit scrawny."

At this point, Frances Fidget-Knickers' tummy rumbled and she said, without thinking, "I'm starving – I really fancy an apple!"

"Did you hear that?" gasped Judge Get-It-Wrong, nearly falling out of his chair. "How very odd!"

"It's not odd at all, your Honour," said Mary, coming to her friend's defence. "She just fancies an apple, that's all."

"You might fancy it, my dear girl," croaked the judge, addressing Frances. "But you can't marry one. It's against the law."

"I meant for consumption," answered Frances. "You know, to eat, your Honour."

Judge Get-It-Wrong slumped back into his chair and sighed. "I'm glad to hear it. For a moment there, I thought you were quite mad."

"Look who's talking," whispered Mary, very quietly.

Judge Get-It-Wrong didn't hear the remark and turned to Mr Never-Won-A-Case. "Right, where's your first witness?"

A click, click, clicking sound rang out, as a small clerk sat just to the side of the judge and started typing away without stopping.

"He's dead," answered the solicitor.

"Ha, is he now?" sighed the judge. "Most interesting, don't you agree?"

"Absolutely, your Honour."

"So, what is it between you and the first witness then?" asked the judge.

Suddenly, Mr Never-Won-A-Case did a little spin and then spoke differently. "Your Honour, about six feet of dirt and a coffin lid." Then he twisted around again and became himself once more.

"Speak up, man!" croaked Judge Get-It-Wrong, wiggling a finger in his ear. "I can't hear a word you're saying!"

The clerk of the court stopped typing briefly and said, "He passed away, your Honour."

"If he's passed this way, then why didn't someone stop him?" boomed the judge, waving his hammer in the air.

"No," hushed the clerk, discreetly, "he's gone to a better place, your Honour."

"Well," cried Judge Get-It-Wrong, "why didn't someone stop him? I'd have had a fiver on the nose in the three-thirty race at Snooze Market!"

"No, no, no, your Honour," said the clerk quickly. "Better. Not betting."

"He'd better not step foot in my courtroom," puffed Judge Get-It-Wrong. "And that's all I've got to say on the matter. You can write that down."

The clerk began to type away at an extraordinary speed, while all the people in the public gallery had by now fallen asleep.

"No!" shouted Judge Get-It-Wrong, banging his hammer down harder than before. "It's a disgrace of biblical proportions! I'll have no sleeping in my courtroom unless I'm doing it first!"

Still the little snoring noises whistled out, as the gallery carried on with their naps.

"He's not all there," commented Mary, much too loudly.

Instantly, at the remark from Mary, everyone awoke with looks of horror. They were now all staring at the two girls.

"You've gone and done it now," cringed Frances.

All this time, Godfrey had been seated with his legs crossed. In encouragement, he sat forward and spoke. "It's going very well, Miss Frances and Miss Mary. You certainly have a way with the legal points of law."

Judge Get-It-Wrong looked down his long, wart-covered nose and cleared his throat for all to hear. "For your information, young lady, I'll have you know that I stood on one leg on top of a stool this morning. And I can also tell you I did it for over thirty minutes without falling off."

Mr Never-Won-A-Case did a little spin and became his alter ego again. He cried out to the public gallery, "Ladies and gentlemen, that means he's well balanced!" He then turned to the twelve jurors and insisted, "It is not our judge who is on trial here!" With another spin, he was his normal self again.

"Well said," sniffed the judge.

Everyone in the courtroom applauded and there were shouts and comments of celebration.

"Best judge in the land!"

"What a fine fellow!"

"Salt of the earth!"

Then it happened. Wham. An almighty slamming of the hammer hushed everyone.

"Who said it? Come on, out with it! Who said 'snort of the earth'?" cried Judge Get-It-Wrong angrily. "I'll have no snorting, sneezing or even wheezing in my court! I could do without a cold! Someone point the culprit out, whoever it was!"

A ratty-looking chap stood up.

The quivering figure stuttered, "I meant no disrespect, your Honour. I said 'salt of the earth', your Lordship."

Judge Get-It-Wrong fumed and spluttered. "There! What did I say? He's only gone and said it again! Disrespectful! Unforgivable! Remove him from my sight this instant!"

Two huge brutes marched over.

They picked up the ratty looking chap.

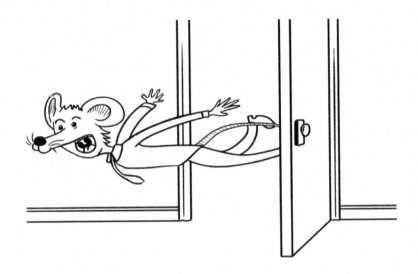

Legs kicking in mid-air, they tossed him from the courtroom.

"Does anyone else feel like interrupting?" huffed Judge Get-It-Wrong.

Nobody said a word.

"I'm waiting," puffed the judge, impatiently.

Still nobody said a word.

"I'm still waiting," repeated the judge, annoyed.

With the feeling that something nasty could happen to all of them, there were loud cheers and waving arms, but no interruptions.

"That's more like it," sniffed Judge Get-It-Wrong.

So no one could hear it but Frances this time, Mary whispered, "Talk about as bonkers as conkers. They're off their heads!"

Mr Never-Won-A-Case shouted over the cheers, "Your Honour! May we continue with the trial?"

In fear of being thrown out like the little ratty chap had just been, everyone stopped with the cheering and sat as still as mice.

Judge Get-It-Wrong said in a huff, "Haven't you started yet?"

"Of course I have, your Honour."

"Well, my boy, you're making a right pig's ear of it," said Judge Get-it-Wrong, putting his hammer down.

"Thank you, your Honour," smiled the solicitor with pride.

"At this rate, your clients will end up guilty, and you'll have a perfect record."

"Thank you again, your Honour," beamed Mr Never-Won-A-Case with delight. "You are too kind."

It was too much for Mary Midget-Mouth to hold in, as she shouted out, "Hold your horses! My friend here, Frances Fidget-Knickers, needs your help! And all you can do is congratulate yourselves for doing nothing to help her! Lucky for us that House has helped so much. But there is only so much House can do! House is a cottage called House, and we could really do with the —"

Slicing through her objections, Judge Get-It-Wrong croaked, while tapping his fingers inquiringly, "A cottage called House, you say?"

"That's right," answered Mary, calming down, quickly adding, "your Honour."

"So, Frances Fidget-Knickers," sniffed Judge Get-It-Wrong. "Who lives with you in this cottage?"

Frances straightened herself as much as she could, considering that there wasn't nearly enough room to do so in the extremely small dock. "Your Honour, as you know, I live in a lovely cottage called House."

"So I've just been told, carry on," instructed the judge.

"Yes, we all live there, your Honour," began Frances, telling her story. "There's my mother, Mrs Windy-Knickers."

"Mrs Windy-Knickers?" gasped Judge Get-It-Wrong, with a shocked look.

"Yes, then there's my father, Mr Rupert Flicker-Knickers," she said, looking even more nervous than before.

"Mr Rupert Flicker-Knickers, you say?" gulped Judge Get-It-Wrong, as the colour drained from his face.

"Yes, and then there's Granddad Sprinkle-Tinkle," cringed Frances, with a sinking feeling of defeat in her stomach.

With that name, the rush of colour raged back and the judge turned a maddening shade of red. "I knew that Granddad Sprinkle-Tinkle was up to something!" he bellowed.

"I think you could be right, your Honour," agreed Mr Never-Won-A-Case.

"I won't be swayed!" boomed the judge, lifting the hammer above his head.

"Of course not, your Honour," smiled Mr Never-Won-A-Case.

"I won't change my mind!" yelled the judge, with his face straining from the words he had just spoken.

"Quite right, your Honour," beamed Mr Never-Won-A-Case, clasping his hands together in eager anticipation of the verdict.

"There's only one choice for it!" screamed Judge Get-It-Wrong, as the hammer came crashing down. "GUILTY!"

"But—" Frances tried to say more.

"Here's your permits," said the judge, handing over the documents and then turning to congratulate Mr Never-Won-A-Case. "Damned fine piece of legal tongue-twisting, my boy; I can see you're going to go far in this profession."

Completely lost as to what had just happened, the two girls looked at one another. They walked out of the dock and up to Godfrey, scratching their heads in confusion. The courtroom was filled with the sounds of cheers once more.

"Well done, Miss Frances and Miss Mary," beamed Godfrey proudly. "I never knew you had it in you. You should take up law."

With the permits in hand, they walked out of the courtroom and straight into the fat man. "This way," he said, marching back up the marbled corridor.

"But we won," stressed Frances.

"That you did," answered the fat man, marching on without looking back.

"So why do we have to follow you?" asked Frances, trotting behind.

"Order of the court," replied the fat man, waving a document. "See for yourself."

Frances took the official piece of paper. At the bottom, Judge Get-It-Wrong had signed it. She handed it to Godfrey and he read it aloud for all to hear.

"On this day ... now what day is it and where has that calendar gone? At the time of ... I've gone and lost my watch ... has anyone seen it? Do hereby give permission for the said two girls named ... blast, now what were they called? To travel by river to Mrs Give-Us-A-Giggle's Shop."

Giving the document back, Godfrey said cautiously, "We have no means of transport."

"That's alright sir," smiled the fat man, hurrying out of the huge building. "We have a vehicle around the corner, manned, ready and waiting to take you there."

CHAPTER 9

THE JOURNEY

A vehicle mounted on two low runners was waiting for them, with four horses ready to go.

They all got into the sledge and the fat man said, "Driver, to the docks, by order of the court, and make it quick."

"Right you are, Sir," nodded the driver, cracking down the whip as they sped away.

Hurtling over the ice, the fat man informed them, "It shouldn't take long."

The driver cracked the whip again and, roared out, "Come on, lads, you can go faster than that!" With a jolt, the sledge shot forwards. Now at full speed, the wind whistled over them and, like the wind, they flew over the snow. Within seconds the chill was beginning to change. One minute later, they swiftly skidded to a stop. The snow and ice had gone. It was warm.

"Here we are, the city of Confectionery," said the driver.

All four made their way to a natural watercourse where a vessel was docked.

The gondola was a fantastic, silky, black colour in appearance. The flat-bottomed boat sat gently in the water and sparkled marvellously.

By contrast, a rather strange chap sat there hanging his head over the side of the boat.

"By order of the court," cried the fat man, eyeing him with dismay. "Mr Swig-It, you've been on the drink again!"

"I haven't," coughed the man, desperately trying to stand while rearranging his threadbare clothes. "Honest!"

"How many have you had, Mr Swig-It?" asked the tubby chap, not believing a word.

"Not too loud, your High Honourableness," hushed Mr Swig-It, holding one hand on his head.

"Well? Out with it!" tutted the chubby fellow.

"I might have had a couple too many last night – after all, I'm a sailor at heart."

"Rum and raisin chocolate bars, no doubt," frowned the fat man, still tutting.

"Now, your Mightiness," hushed Mr Swig-It, acting innocently. "You wouldn't want a humble servant of the court to be putting up with a horrid empty feeling in his stomach?"

"Look at the state of him," said Mary.

"Thank you, little lady," sniffed Mr Swig-It. "Kind of you to notice. It's taken years of hard work to look this bad. Mind you, there was a time when I thought I wasn't going to make it. Trying times, troubling days, would turn your liver inside out if I told you."

"Sir," began Frances, getting Mr Swig-It's attention.

"Sir," she said, smiled Mr Swig-It. "No one's ever called me 'Sir' before. I'll be liking you, little miss."

"You don't drink rum and raisin bars of chocolate," she went on to say, knowledgably.

"Now, missy, depends on the brand," answered Mr Swig-It. "You wouldn't want to go putting me through torture by making me munch away on solids … when it would be so much easier to drink it, now, would we?"

"He's got a point, Miss Frances," said Godfrey, sniffing the air, "and a highly potent one at that."

With the wonderful thought, Mr Swig-It had gone into a daydream, rubbing his tummy and sighing, "Fantabulous."

"Snap out of it, man!" insisted the fat man, stepping forwards. "Here is a court order. It's ordering you to take these three people to Mrs Give-Us-A-Giggle's shop."

The sailor almost lost control of his balance.

With a sudden sharp intake of breath, he gasped, "I haven't been that way for years. Rough terrain and treacherous waters getting there; don't know if this here gondola is up to the job. What's in it for me?"

"There's no bonus in it," replied the overweight man, "but Judge Get-It-Wrong has ordered a huge chest of chocolates for you on your return."

"Rum and raisin?" asked Mr Swig-It.

"The finest brand, ready and waiting for your collection, when you get back," smiled the fat man

"All aboard!" shouted Mr Swig-It.

Slowly but surely, Godfrey, Frances and Mary stepped aboard, and a peculiar floating sensation took over.

"Whoops-a-daisy!" Godfrey called out, slipping slightly. "Mind yourselves, Miss Frances and Miss Mary. Now that we have come this far, we don't want any accidents."

"Steady yourselves, shipmates!" cried Mr Swig-It, taking out a melted bar of chocolate. "Don't want to be upsetting me drinking arm and the rich rewards on me return!"

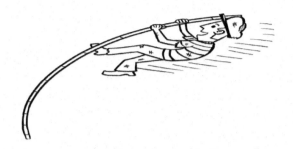

"You should go on the wagon," suggested Frances, knowing that this meant to stop drinking.

"These here sea legs of mine are no good for wagon train journeys, young missy," explained Mr Swig-It. "I tried it once and ended up getting land-sickness."

"Where are the sails?" asked Mary. "Come to think of it, where are the oars?"

"There are no oars on this vessel and I don't need any sails either," answered Mr Swig-It. "Things work a bit different in these parts."

"Do they?" asked Mary.

"How so?" asked Frances, as the sailor looked over his boat, clearly searching for something.

Then he took up an extremely long pole, which looked like you could pole vault with it. "This is a gondola of me own design." Bending the pole, he cried out, "All ashore that's going ashore!"

The fat man waved goodbye.

Mr Swig-It ran to the front of the boat and pushed down the pole with such a force that it bent almost in two. When the pole would bend no more, he was sent up in the air, still holding onto the other end. He was now vaulting over their heads. "Who needs sails?" he cried. "This is much more fun!"

"Can't anyone be normal in this world?" sighed Mary, disbelievingly.

"How long do you think it will take?" enquired Godfrey, referring to the journey ahead.

Mr Swig-It looked down at all three sitting in the gondola and shouted, "About fifteen seconds a stroke!"

Frances Fidget-Knickers couldn't help but laugh at Mary's perplexed look of disbelief as Mr Swig-It landed skilfully.

He was now standing at the back end of the gondola, and tossed an empty sweet wrapper over the side.

"Mr Swig-It," cried Frances Fidget-Knickers, "you're a litterbug, doing things like that!"

"Don't be preposterous," laughed the scraggy figure of a man, getting ready to undo another delicious chocolate bar. "I look nothing like one." He pointed to the water below, where a swarm of insects had descended upon the wrapper to carry it off. "You wouldn't want me to be depriving them of their meal, now, would we?"

"I suppose not," blinked Frances, scratching her head and somewhat puzzled by the sight.

Mary, still looking confused, mumbled her words, "I wonder what he meant."

"Miss Mary, speak up, and to whom are you referring?" asked Godfrey, steadying himself. "Could you be more specific, or give us a clue?"

"Judge Get-It-Wrong," Mary answered, lifting her voice for all to hear.

"About what?" Frances asked.

"Your grandfather," replied Mary, staring across the water. "You know, Granddad Sprinkle-Tinkle."

All of a sudden, Mr Swig-It choked on the chocolate trickling down his throat, and spluttered, "Not that old bulldog chewing a wasp?"

"So you've heard of him?" said Godfrey.

"Bulldog Sprinkle-Tinkle, the scourge of these here lands," shuddered Mr Swig-It. "Who hasn't?"

"Bulldog?" said Frances Fidget-Knickers.

"That would be one of his many nicknames, Miss Frances and Miss Mary."

"Bad things happened before that man was banished," sniffed Mr Swig-It, saving some of the chocolate that had run down his top.

"That they were," sighed Godfrey, letting out a large amount of air.

"Thank God for Mr Shed-Lock-Groans," insisted Mr Swig-It, admiringly. "If it weren't for him, we'd all be dead in our beds at night, or possibly the morning, or even worse."

"What could be worse than being dead?" asked Mary.

Stuffing his face, Mr Swig-It said nervously, after gulping, "NO CHOCOLATE!"

"Shed-Lock-Groans," puzzled Frances. "I've never heard of him."

"Don't you mean Ship-Lock-Groans?" smiled Godfrey.

"They tried him, but he was always sailing off to see the world," answered the sailor, licking his fingers.

"Of course, I remember now," replied Godfrey. "Nobody has ever heard or seen of him since."

"That's what the papers say," stated Mr Swig-It. "So they needed a person who was a specialist in his field."

"That he is," agreed Godfrey.

"Someone who had worked their way up from the very bottom."

"That he did," Godfrey said with great pride.

"Someone who had started at the end of the garden."

"Why, it's so obvious when you think about it," beamed Godfrey from ear to ear.

"Someone who had begun his career in sheds."

"We all have to start somewhere in life," smiled Godfrey with admiration.

Suddenly, Mr Swig-It darted to the other end of the boat and pushed down with the pole once again. Again, he was sailing over their heads.

"I don't understand!" shouted Frances.

Mr Swig-It's hands were all slippery from his finger-licking, and he started to slide. "Hold on just one moment, young missy!" he cried, struggling to retain his grip. "I'm having a bit of a problem up here!"

The three of them watched him struggle. Mr Swig-It's legs did a scissor grip so tight that he had time to lap up the very slippery chocolate from his hands.

"Mr Shed-Lock-Groans is a house detective," he said. "Not just any old house detective but the best house detective in the whole wide world."

With that, he landed.

"Golly!" exclaimed Mary Midget-Mouth.

"Exactly," smiled the sailor, searching the deck. "Who else could they possibly use?"

Now with her mouth in gear and brain out of action, Mary gabbled, "Granddad Sprinkle-Tinkle must have done something really bad, like murdering people in their homes and chopping them up. Maybe he even buried them alive."

"Thanks for the thought," said Frances sarcastically.

"I didn't mean anything by it," Mary replied apologetically.

"Just as well," said Mr Swig-It, taking out yet another bar of chocolate, "because she's wrong. Maiming, pillaging and abduction are all commonplace around these parts. What Granddad Sprinkle-Tinkle did was unforgivable."

"I don't think that these young ears are ready for such stories," shuddered Godfrey, trying to stop the conversation.

"They're not stories," he insisted. "It's all documented from the trial. If any of you don't believe me, you can read it for yourselves."

"Believe what?" asked Frances Fidget-Knickers insistently.

"Should I go on, shipmate?" Mr Swig-It asked Godfrey.

With a worried look, he answered, "I'm not sure."

"They're going to find out one way or another. At least this way you can correct me if I'm wrong."

Godfrey thought long and hard before saying, "In that case I will keep a check on things, please proceed."

"Well, now, shipmates," continued Mr Swig-It, running to the front of the gondola and pushing down the pole again. "This be a true story of a long time ago."

The pole fired Mr Swig-It back into the air. They all looked up at him.

Passing over their heads, he said, "There were rumours at the time of a secret group of people. No one dared believe the gossip. They were far too ghastly to imagine, but people whisper … and whispers get blown out of all proportions. Made me think at the time I'd be safer at the bottom of the ocean with old Davy Crockett."

Frances watched with eagle eyes as the sailor landed and took another chocolate bar out of a small box.

Mr Swig-It rubbed his chin and went on explaining. "The top brass at the Department of Sorcery were flummoxed. So they called in the army, air force and navy, along with the intelligence service and police force. For years they ended up at dead ends, unable to solve the crimes of this secret cult of followers. Then some bright spark in the police force suggested they use Mr Shed-Lock-Groans, the greatest house detective who had ever lived."

"So the crime was solved in a jiffy," interrupted Mary, looking pleased with herself.

"Not so, little missy," panted Mr Swig-It, running back to the front of the gondola and repeating the pole-pushing.

Looking up, Frances asked, "So who was it?"

Looking down, Mr Swig-It explained, "I'm coming to that bit."

Mr Swig-It landed.

Godfrey smiled. "He's spot on so far, Miss Frances and Miss Mary."

"As I was saying," breathed Mr Swig-It, in between guzzling down another chocolate bar, "Mr Shed-Lock-Groans had to infiltrate his way into the secret gang. This wasn't easy, not when you're an upstanding gentleman like the good fellow I'm talking about. At first he had to disappear completely and learn the ways of the jackal. He had to become as cunning as a fox."

The gondola slowed a little and Mr Swig-It was off with the pole-pushing once more.

"Bet that wasn't an easy thing to do?" said Frances, looking up.

Passing over their heads, he answered, "You're absolutely right, and that's why it took Mr Shed-Lock-Groans years to even begin to be trusted. Once he had gained their confidence, he began with the collecting of information and keeping records on the whereabouts of this secret band of brothers."

"So they arrested them all, then?" asked Mary, watching Mr Swig-It land.

"Not so, young missy," he sighed, swigging yet another bar of chocolate.

"But he had the information they needed," said Frances.

"Only on who they were, but not on what they did," answered the sailor.

"Absolutely correct," agreed Godfrey.

"That I am, shipmate," smiled Mr Swig-It, before going on with the tale of evil. "You see, me good people, there was no evidence, only speculation. You can't arrest someone on hearsay. You need hard facts."

"How did Mr Shed-Lock-Groans manage to get them?" asked Frances.

"There was a breakthrough," he answered. "A fine figure of a cottage spoke up."

"That wouldn't be House by any chance, would it?" asked Mary.

"Which one?" replied Mr Swig-It, becoming a little bit wobblier on his legs from eating too many rum and raisin chocolate bars.

"Mr and Mrs Flicker-Knickers' cottage called House," answered Mary.

"Blow me down with a feather!" cried Mr Swig-It. "If that don't be the very same cottage called House that I'm speaking about!" He looked deep into the distance and froze for a few moments, fear washing over his face.

"Are you alright?" asked Godfrey, worried.

"White waters!" cried Mr Swig-It.

"Oh no!" gasped Godfrey.

"What's the problem?" quizzed Frances and Mary simultaneously.

"Rapids!" cried Mr Swig-It.

Then Mr Swig-It took three chocolate bars out and gulped them all down as quickly as he could. "I might as well make the most of it, because I might not get another chance to taste the sweet delicious rum and raisin ever again!"

All three watched the sailor running around the gondola as though he had just seen a ghost. Then he began with the instructions.

"You do this and I'll do that. He does this and she does that. After which, she'll get this and he'll do that. I'll be here doing this while you're over there doing that. She gets this and he'll get that. After which, we'll all need a chair. Right, is everyone clear on this and that?"

"Perfect instructions, Captain," smiled Godfrey, congratulating Mr Swig-It.

"I haven't got a clue what he meant," stressed Mary.

"Nor me," whispered Frances. "It made no sense whatsoever."

"No time to go through it again!" cried Mr Swig-It, as the gondola started to rock.

"Don't you realise?" Mary called out, as the gondola tipped from side to side. "We didn't understand!"

"Maybe you should learn to listen more carefully than you did before," panicked Mr Swig-It, "as the waters in these parts have had a wizard's spell cast over them. Cursed, I tell you."

Up in front, a mass of folding water turned over and over, and piercing through the waves were large rocks. The torrent started to pick up speed. The further they went down the ravine, the faster they became. Deep, narrow gorges, with their steep sides, echoed with the roaring sounds of fast-running water. Overwhelmingly, the tormented and powerful waves crashed into the gondola.

"We're going to sink!" cried Godfrey.

"No, we're not!" shouted Mr Swig-It. "This vessel is made of rubber!"

"Are you sure?" cried out Godfrey.

The force of a crushing wave smashed down with all its might and hit the front of the gondola. Mr Swig-It, standing at the other end, was sent flying upwards and into the air.

"Absolutely!" he yelled.

"Mr Swig-It!" shouted Godfrey, staring into the sky. "Will you come down at once! A captain's place is with his vessel!"

Frances and Mary held on for dear life.

"Can't!" shouted Mr Swig-it, watching a wave. "You'll have to come up to meet me!"

From his flying position, Mr Swig-It saw an enormous wave heading their way.

The gondola vanished for a split second and was then tossed upwards from the force of the water.

Up, up, up it went, and then they were all together again.

"Hold on tight, shipmates!" cried Mr Swig-It.

"We are!" Frances Fidget-Knickers cried out.

Stuffing another bar of chocolate down his throat, Mr Swig-It shouted, "A bad storm approaching!"

"I thought that we were already in one!" shouted Mary Midget-Mouth.

"So did I!" shouted Frances Fidget-Knickers to her friend.

"He's lost the plot!" yelled Mary back to Frances.

"I'll second that!" hollered Frances to Mary, before something unbelievable suddenly happened.

Rotating winds grabbed hold of them and they were sent spinning through a funnel-shaped cloud of spray. It was as though they were spinning down a white-knuckle roller coaster ride made from water.

Faster and faster they went – up and down and all around in what seemed to take forever, until they finally splashed down safely.

The bay was calm and Mr Swig-It praised the two girls. "Darned best bit of seamanship I ever did see, and you said you didn't listen to me instructions. I think you were having a joke on poor old Mr Swig-It here."

"No, we weren't," sighed Frances in relief.

"That goes for me too," trembled Mary, still shaking from the shocking experience.

"You must be naturals, like ducks to water," smiled Mr Swig-It, admiringly.

"By Lord, is there nothing you two girls can't do?" cried Godfrey. "If it wasn't for your help, we'd have been goners for sure!"

Frances rushed her words, "But all we did was fall forwards and backwards and sideways and any other way you could think of."

"That may be so, young missy," munched Mr Swig-It, chewing another chocolate bar, "but you did it with expert timing."

"He'll end up getting fatter than an elephant, eating all that chocolate," said Mary.

"That may be so, young miss," grinned Mr Swig-It, between chews, "but I'll not argue with someone who far exceeds my sailing skills. It would be against the laws of the sea."

A beautiful, tranquil river lay before them as they sailed on, while behind them were the distant reminders of fast-moving water. As they moved downstream, the countryside began to change.

"So what happened?" asked Frances, addressing Mr Swig-It. "You know, about House?"

"No time for yesterday's news," he said, starting the preparations. "We're landing in a minute."

Mary's exploring look gave way to a mumble, "Who would want to live here?"

There were no trees to be seen. There was no grass. In fact, there was no sign of life anywhere. There was nothing but an emptiness of sand and rock.

"Mrs Give-Us-A-Giggle lives just over the horizon," said Mr Swig-It, shovelling another chocolate bar into his mouth.

The gondola slid gently to a stop and nestled on the sand bank just halfway out of the water. "All ashore who's going ashore!" shouted Mr Swig-It.

The three of them stepped off the boat and onto the sand, and then Frances asked, "What happened with House?"

"I'd like to stop and chat, young missy, but I've got treasures to get back for," smiled Mr Swig-It, pushing the gondola free and sailing off. "Chocolate ones at that!"

"What about House?" shouted Frances Fidget-Knickers, running into the water.

"Now, young missy, there's someone more able than I to tell you," called Mr Swig-It, searching himself. "Blast! I've gone and run out of rum and raisin!"

"Who would that be?" shouted Frances, backing out of the river.

A distant cry came floating back from Mr Swig-It. "Ask Mrs Give-Us-A-Giggle! She knows more than I do! She worked with Mr Shed-Lock-Groans!"

CHAPTER 10

THE SHOP

It was quiet. The only sound was the gentle waves breaking on the shore. The barren wasteland carried on up a slight slope and away from the sandy beach.

"This is a place unsuitable for living in," sighed Godfrey. "Talk about being caught between a rock and a hard place."

Frances shook her feet one by one and said, "If we don't get a move on soon, the sun will give us heatstroke, then the feverish condition will end up making us weak. We'll all end up emaciated and unable to go on."

Mary gazed over the barren land and a question fell from her lips, "Frances, you've been eating a dictionary for breakfast again. You should learn to get out more often. Emaciated – what does that mean?"

"Emaciated means to become thin and weak," replied Frances Fidget-Knickers.

"I was right," said Mary, with a smirk on her face. "You know what I think – you're in danger of becoming a bookworm."

"We haven't got time for this idle chit-chat," stomped the rodent, marching off. "Mr Swig-It said to go over the horizon to Mrs Give-Us-A-Giggle's shop. And it looks like quite a long walk from here."

As they walked along, their feet sank into the sand. With each passing step, it was becoming harder and harder to pick their feet up. The sun burned down on them, making it even more difficult to go on.

"Godfrey," said Frances, beginning her question, "do you really know why we were banished?"

"Of course I do," he answered, trudging on.

113

"So what happened, then? I'd love to know!" asked Mary, butting in.

"I'm not allowed to say," Godfrey answered, taking heavy steps.

"Why ever not?" puffed Frances Fidget-Knickers, breathing heavily.

"I've sworn an oath on the good book never to talk about it," informed Godfrey, pounding into the sand with forceful stepping movements.

Proceeding gradually, they made their way out of the sunken enclosure. Below them was a neglected town of ramshackle buildings that had long seen better days.

"Do you mean on the Bible?" asked Mary.

"Yes," answered the rat, dusting himself off.

"Well, that's that then," insisted Mary, kicking her foot into the sand. "You can't go against the Holy Church."

"We can ask Mrs Give-Us-A-Giggle!" cried Frances, running on in front. "Last one down is a baboon-faced idiot!"

"It's not going to be me!" shouted her friend, chasing after.

"First's the worst!" cried Godfrey, scampering at their heels.

"Second's the best!" squealed Frances, speeding up.

"Third's the one with the hairy chest!" shouted Mary Midget-Mouth, watching Godfrey dash by, before adding, "I guess that's me, then!"

In no time at all, they were approaching the deserted town, and they stopped just before it. Taking time to regain themselves, they walked along apprehensively. A rolling bundle of weed tumbled down the street.

Mary watched the rolling plant and laughed, "Look at that. Even the tumbleweed has packed its suitcases and given up on this place."

Frances searched the rows of empty buildings, looking for Mrs Give-Us-A-Giggle's shop.

"Miss Frances and Miss Mary, it's been years since I was last here," smiled Godfrey, looking around. "Nothing has changed. Still the same – oh, I'm so glad."

Then, for some strange reason, the rodent lifted his cane as though to greet someone and said, "Good day to you."

The two girls exchanged glances.

"Too much sun," whispered Frances.

"Fried his brains," replied Mary softly.

"Come along, Miss Frances and Miss Mary," said Godfrey, stepping to one side as though something was in the way. "We haven't got all day. I've got to be thinking of getting you home soon. By the way, do stop whispering – it's very impolite."

They walked on past an old, empty butcher's shop, baker's shop, clothes shop and several more derelict buildings, before they finally stopped.

"Here it is," announced Godfrey, proudly opening the door. "It's just as I remembered it."

Two very excited girls rushed in. Once inside, the excitement turned to shock.

"It's empty!" cried Frances Fidget-Knickers, disappointed.

All around, broken, dusty shelves lay in heaps on the floor. Scattered throughout the shop, mounds of old papers and plastic packets lay rotting, while in between them, mouldy clothes gave the air a musky smell. The counter was riddled with woodworm and falling to pieces. To one end of the counter sat a little metal cash register. Different tins of all sorts had been crushed and left to rust on the floor.

"What a mess," commented Mary.

Godfrey tapped the counter and talked into thin air. "My compliments, Mrs Give-Us-A-Giggle, for maintaining such a well-kept establishment."

Frances and Mary pulled faces at one another, as if to say 'he's gone mad from the heat of the sun'.

As if by magic, when they turned around again, a lady stood behind the counter.

"Hello, me dears," she beamed, invitingly.

Godfrey beamed back the biggest smile he could muster.

Frances and Mary didn't know what to do, as they jumped in surprise.

The woman behind the counter put her hands down on the glass and pressed into it. Leaning over, she peered through the brown, horn-rimmed spectacles sitting halfway down her nose. The lady had the most sparkling light blue eyes and crystal-clear complexion. She had the blackest hair there was, and it was tied in a bun, fixed behind her head with knitting needles. She was also very tall and very plump.

As she spoke, her voice resonated beautifully and flowed with gentleness. "I'm Mrs Give-Us-A-Giggle, me dears."

Frances and Mary, still a little shocked, stood still.

"Now then, Miss Frances and Miss Mary, is that any way to greet someone?" asked Godfrey, turning to the creator of hocus-pocus and apologising. "Sorry about that, you'll have to excuse them – I think the sun's gone to their heads."

"Well, we can't have that now, can we?" tutted Mrs Give-Us-A-Giggle, clicking her fingers twice.

Between the moment the sound of clicking fingers started and the time at which the sound faded, the shop transformed itself.

"Wowee!" gasped both girls.

The shop was now a marvellous place, filled with wonderments and trickery. Oodles of stuff with wondrous fillings now crammed into every available space. Shelves that had sat on the floor now hung on walls, filled with all kinds of packets. Hanging overhead were witch's hats and broomsticks, wizard's clocks and masks of ghoulish monsters. Draped down the walls hung outfits of phantoms, ghosts, goblins and trolls with hideous grins. In the shop window stood a mummy, wrapped in bleached bandages. The till now looked brand new, and the counter gleamed and shone magnificently, with a tray of drinks sat on top.

"There we are," said the maker of impossible feats, approvingly. "That's much better. Now then, how about some refreshments?"

"How did you do that?" asked Frances Fidget-Knickers.

"Miss Frances and Miss Mary," smiled Godfrey proudly. "You can't come into a joke shop and expect for someone who runs it to be normal."

"You can't?" spluttered Frances.

"No, you can't, Miss Frances," replied Godfrey. "Mrs Give-Us-A-Giggle is a white witch."

"So what's the difference between white and black witches?" asked Mary.

"Evil," answered the tall lady. "Now, how about that drink, me dears?"

With only two cups sat on the tray, Frances said, "What about Godfrey?"

"Not for me, Miss Frances," he smiled, knowingly. "I'm trying to watch my weight."

"But it's only lemonade," said Mary, looking into the half-filled cups.

The magical maker of wonderful things topped them up with what looked like lemonade, and slid them over to the two girls. "There you go, me dears. Enjoy!"

The first sip was taken by Frances. As she did so, she looked almost too flabbergasted to speak.

Dumbfounded, Frances Fidget-Knickers gasped, "It's not lemonade! It's vanilla ice cream … no, wait a minute … it's banana ice cream … now it's changed to tutti-frutti … blimey ... it's now mint choc-chip!"

Mary sipped from her cup and gabbled, "Mine's blueberry pie and whipped cream … it's changing … apple strudel and custard ... it's changing again … Ooh, my favourite, death by chocolate!"

From the first sip, there was no stopping them, as the cups were refilled time and time again.

"It's strawberries and cream!" cried Frances.

"It's white chocolate-covered toffee apples!" shouted Mary.

"It's toffee fudge surprise!" screamed Frances delightedly.

"It's all my birthdays rolled up into one!" yelled Mary, uncontrollably.

When all the shouting and screaming had died down, and Frances and Mary could drink no more, they sighed contentedly, their tummies pushed out.

"I'm stuffed," belched Frances Fidget-Knickers.

"Me too," burped Mary Midget-Mouth.

Mrs Give-Us-A-Giggle said with a smile, "I'm not surprised. What you've just had is food drink, and ten helpings at that."

"See," said Godfrey. "I told you I was watching my weight."

Just then, the door opened and in stepped a lady.

"Hello, Mrs Gabble-Gob," smiled Mrs Give-Us-A-Giggle. "Isn't it nice to see Godfrey again?"

"I wouldn't mind seeing Godfrey," huffed Mrs Gabble-Gob, "but it's strangers I don't like."

"You don't have to worry about these two little things, me dear," said the whitest of white witches. "They're with Godfrey."

The rodent quickly introduced them. "My dear Mrs Gabble-Gob, how lovely to see you again – you're looking well. This is Miss Frances and Miss Mary."

"How do you do?" nodded Mrs Gabble-Gob to both of them. "I'll not be stopping, good day to you all." She turned and walked straight through the door without even opening it.

"She's a ghost!" cried Frances Fidget-Knickers, her mouth nearly hitting the floor.

"Of course she's a ghost," replied Mrs Give-Us-A-Giggle. "What else would she be? After all, she does live in a ghost town."

With that, Mrs Give-Us-A-Giggle passed through the counter and up to the shop window.

"Blimey!" exclaimed Mary. "You're a ghost as well?"

119

"No, I'm a white witch," answered the performer of spell-craft, looking out into the street. "Looks like Mrs Gabble-Gob has been gossiping and told everyone that it's safe to come out."

Outside, the town had transformed. Where once stood old rundown properties, fantastic buildings, painted in many different colours, now replaced them. The streets had become busy, with lots of people hustling and bustling their way through the day. Sounds of happy-go-lucky ghosts drifted into the shop.

"Right, me dears," said Mrs Give-Us-A-Giggle. "Now that everyone is happy with you being here, we can get on with doing some business."

Godfrey saw the looks of uneasiness on Frances' and Mary's faces. "Don't worry about them, they're decent townsfolk. They won't pester you."

Frances felt encouraged by this and said, "I'm looking for two particular tricks."

"Now, me dears," sighed the kindest of witches, "I didn't mean that. So what would you like to know about Granddad Sprinkle-Tinkle?"

Naturally, Frances Fidget-Knickers' keen mind wanted to know more about the tricks, but she asked instead, "How did you know my next question would be about my grandfather?"

Mrs Give-Us-A-Giggle answered in a long-winded kind of way. "Oh, me dears, it's just a white witch trick of mind-reading, and it all started when I was working for a gentleman called Mr Shed-Lock-Groans."

"We've heard of him," said Mary.

"Have you now, me dears?"

"Yes," replied Frances. "Mr Swig-It told us some of the story."

"Did he, now, me dears?" smiled Mrs Give-Us-A-Giggle. "Shall I fill in the gaps?"

"Please, if you don't mind?" Frances asked.

"Well, we'd been undercover for over four and a half years, trying to work our way into the inner circle," began the white witch, raising an eyebrow. "At first, most of our days were spent doing menial tasks. We would go around plundering and stealing from villages."

"Did you kill anyone?" asked Mary, interested.

"No," answered the enchantment-maker, politely. "You're forgetting that I'm a white witch – we do not go around killing or hurting any living thing."

"But you said you pillaged and stole from villages," insisted Mary.

"That I did, young lady," replied Mrs Give-Us-A-Giggle, falling silent.

"Please go on," prompted Frances.

"Righty-ho, me dears," sighed Mrs Give-Us-A-Giggle. "Mr Shed-Lock-Groans needed someone who had magical abilities."

"That would be you, then?" said Mary.

"Yes, me dear, that is why I went undercover with him," explained the white witch. "All the time I was with him, I could make it look like we were chopping people up and murdering them. For, you see, I had cast a powerful spell over us that made it look so."

Frances and Mary listened intensely.

As though a great weight had been lifted, the spell-caster of good magic sighed long and hard, before going on with the tale of wrongdoing. "The wicked worshippers possessed the strongest form of black magic, and they had cast an even more powerful spell over themselves for protection."

Frances popped out a question, "What did you do?"

"There wasn't much I could do," she sighed, rocking her head from side to side. "It was much too strong for my abilities to break."

"How did you overcome it?" asked Frances.

"We secretly stayed in touch with the authorities and kept them informed by way of House."

"So you just told House – I mean, my cottage called House?"

"That's right," answered Mrs Give-Us-A-Giggle. "Houses are incorruptible. They are immune to black magic of any kind. So we could trust them and, for years, messages went back and forth."

"So if hurting someone isn't a very serious crime in these parts, then what is?" asked Mary.

"Arson!" gasped Mrs Give-Us-A-Giggle, with a shudder. "People who go around deliberately setting fire to Houses."

"But that's not as bad as all the other stuff," said Mary, insistently.

"It's every bit as bad. Even more serious than all the other crimes," declared the maker of witchcraft. "Houses are the oldest living beings that are known to this world, and we are taught to respect our elders."

"So," began Frances, "was my grandfather an arsonist?"

"Afraid so," sighed Mrs Give-Us-A-Giggle. "But not just any old arsonist – he was the head of the organisation. He told the followers where and when to set fire to any House that didn't side with him."

"How could he?" gasped Frances Fidget-Knickers, disgusted.

"What a rotten toad!" added Mary Midget-Mouth.

"How did he get caught?" asked Frances, wanting to know more.

Godfrey came in at that point and said, "Your cottage sealed their fate."

"That's absolutely right," agreed the white witch. "But not before they had their revenge on the cottage and set fire to House."

"I feel very angry with my grandfather's horrid behaviour."

"Just imagine what it would feel like to be burned alive," shuddered Mary.

Mrs Give-Us-A-Giggle looked at them all. "Unknown to those wicked followers, I had cast a spell over House. The enchantment made it appear as though the building was going up in smoke."

"Good for you," smiled Frances, with a punch of victory.

"Not so fast with the celebration, me dear," stressed Mrs Give-Us-A-Giggle. "When they found out that they had been tricked, those evil people took hammers to the cottage and smashed the walls in."

"Oh my goodness!" exclaimed Mary, shocked.

"It was touch-and-go for House," shuddered the white witch. "It nearly killed the poor little cottage."

"Oh no," said Frances sympathetically.

"Luckily," smiled Mrs Give-Us-A-Giggle, "House pulled through."

With tears welling in her eyes Frances sighed heavily. "Poor old House, why ever did House let my grandfather live with us?"

"It's not up to House who lives there," stated the conjurer of bewitchments. "That was up to your mother and father, for they were the ones who had signed the contract, giving them the rights to move anyone in."

"I'm really glad we played those tricks on him now," Mary said.

"That reminds me," smiled the white witch. "What tricks would you like to take back with you?"

"Well," sniffed Frances, wiping her eyes, "I'd like itching powder and some fake blood."

Mrs Give-Us-A-Giggle looked oddly at her. "I've never heard of them, but I do have two items that are pretty nasty."

With that, she shouted over to the shop window. "Mr Whinge-Pot, would you kindly go out to the storeroom and fetch the Nibbling-Nibblers – oh, and the bar of soap please!"

All of a sudden, the mummy started to move.

It had come to life and moaned, "Oh, my aching back, I've been stuck in that position for ages. Really, I should get a different line of work, but who would employ a ghost? All they ever do is run away when I ask for a job."

"Jumping toadstools!" cried Frances, jumping out of her skin.

"Bejesus!" yelped Mary, clinging onto her friend.

"I thought you were a dummy!" exclaimed Frances Fidget-Knickers.

"Don't be silly," sniffed Mr Whinge-Pot. "I'm a mummy, not a harlequin. I'll have you know I was mummified in ancient Egyptian times. On this occasion, I shall forgive that remark."

Mr Whinge-Pot walked out the back and soon returned with a jar. Inside the glass container sat a very hairy something.

"What is it?" asked Frances, peering into the jar.

"It's a Nibble-Back," answered Godfrey uneasily. "Nasty little blighter."

With fascination, Frances and Mary looked closer. The Nibble-Back sat perfectly still.

"Miss Frances and Miss Mary, please be careful," insisted Godfrey. "You need to be an expert to handle such a creature."

"He's perfectly right," agreed Mrs Give-Us-A-Giggle, taking the jar. "Please leave the soap on the counter. Thank you, Mr Whinge-Pot, that will be all."

"I'll leave you to it, then," grumbled the moaning mummy, whinging on the way back to the shop window. "My aching feet, my aching back … mind you, it could be worse, but I'll never know."

Stepping back into place, he became still and lifeless again.

"Now, me dears," wheezed Mrs Give-Us-A-Giggle, shaking the jar. "Don't be frightened, I'm only making it cross. The madder it gets, the better the result will be."

Inside the jar, the ball of hair puffed up.

"Looks like it's working," said Mrs Give-Us-A-Giggle with a smile.

Tiny little creatures, identical to the Nibble-Back, fell out of its fur.

"There they are," panted the white witch in delight.

"Are they Nibble-Backs?" asked Mary, looking deep into the jar.

"No, me dears," smiled Mrs Give-Us-A-Giggle. "They're the young of a Nibble-Back. Nibbling-Nibblers, to be precise – they eat almost anything. Mind out the way while I put them in a bag for you."

"Won't they eat through that?" asked Frances.

"Paper and clothes are about the only things these little darlings don't eat," she replied, starting to tip them into a brown bag. "Now, I've got to do this properly or we'll all be taking a bath."

There was a silence as the tiny Nibbling-Nibblers fell inside. Quickly the bag was sealed. From time to time, it would move sharply as the creatures inside tried to escape.

"Why a bath?" asked Mary.

"A bath stops them doing funny things," she answered, putting the packet down on the glass counter.

Frances inspected the brown bag as it twitched, "So the water stops them?"

"No, me dears," smiled Mrs Give-Us-A-Giggle, placing the soap next to the bag. "This stops them eating. Mind you, it does have a funny side effect, but it's the only thing that works. How I wish I could be there when you play these tricks. I just don't have the time. Maybe I might make some time one day and give you a visit."

Godfrey dug into his pocket and asked, "How much do we owe you, Mrs Give-Us-A-Giggle?"

"About two thimbles and a plaster," she answered, shaking her hand. "All I keep doing lately is pricking my fingers."

"Look at that, the exact amount," exclaimed Godfrey, pulling two thimbles and a plaster out.

"Hold on, we don't have a balloon or a gondola," stressed Frances Fidget-Knickers. "How are we going to get back?"

Mrs Give-Us-A-Giggle smiled. "Well, me dears, you could try that door over there."

Godfrey, Frances and Mary said their goodbyes and walked over to the door. They pushed it open and walked through it.

Again, something fantastic happened; they were all back in the cellar before they knew it.

"Miss Frances and Miss Mary," said Godfrey, "I wish you well and good luck with the tricks."

With that, he was gone.

CHAPTER 11

THE SURPRISE

Both girls started to climb the cobbled stairs.

Frances stretched out her arm and gently stroked the wall. "House, I never knew. I'm so sorry."

Mary did the same. "What a brave House you are."

The cottage shook. "IT'S ALL IN THE PAST."

Frances Fidget-Knickers held the bag up and cried, "One for all and all for one!"

"Hang on a minute," said Mary. "Don't you mean two for one and none for us?"

The cottage quivered ever so slightly. "VERY FUNNY," chuckled House. "GOOD LUCK."

It was just as they stood in the hallway, with the results of the journey in Frances Fidget-Knickers' hand, that it happened.

As soon as Granddad Sprinkle-Tinkle spotted them, he was at it. "Where do you think you two have been all this time?" he grumbled, holding a bath towel around his middle.

The bag of magic tricks was hidden out of sight behind Frances Fidget-Knickers' back. "Playing in the cellar," she answered.

Granddad Sprinkle-Tinkle, his pencil neck stretching, peered suspiciously at them. "Frances, what are you hiding behind your back?"

"Nothing," she fibbed, staring at her feet. "Honest."

"You're lying," hissed her horrid grandfather, his eyes blazing fiendishly. "Show me your hands – and that goes for you, too, Mary Midget-Mouth."

Somehow, before Mary even knew it, her hands were out and in front of her.

"Keep them there where I can see them," he insisted.

Now with his full attention on his granddaughter, he repeated, "Show me your hands, girly!"

Instantly, she held out her right hand, while all the time holding the bag in her left. "See!" she said, smugly.

"Did you think I was born yesterday?" snorted Granddad Sprinkle-Tinkle. "What about the other one?"

Frances slid her right hand back, changed the package from left to right and held out her left arm. "See! Nothing in that either!" she said, trying to sound convincing.

Mary, with her arms still stretched out, stood there shaking like a baby's rattle.

The nastiest and meanest grandfather bellowed, "Do you take me for an idiot? I want to see both hands out here at the same time!"

Mary almost fainted.

Cool as a cucumber, Frances Fidget-Knickers' brain went into overdrive. "Very well," she said, returning the left hand behind her back.

"Hurry up," he growled.

Now that both limbs were hidden, Frances quickly folded the bag over and into the waistband on her jeans. "There you go, Granddad, see? I told you I had nothing," she said, showing both hands and grinning secretly inside her head.

"You're up to something," sniffed Granddad Sprinkle-Tinkle, defeated. "I can smell it."

Looking at Mary, he snorted, "I have a very good nose for mischievous children. All children give off the same wretched stench. Right now, both of you don't smell too good. If I find out what it is you two are up to, you'll both be in serious trouble. Mark my words, or else I'll be putting me fingers up your nose and ripping out your eyeballs."

This was not the time to celebrate the victory of their deception, so Frances just said, "Right you are, Granddad."

"If I had me way, I'd handcuff both of you around the washing pole," he cursed. "The only reason I don't is because I'm far too nice a person. Now, where's me clothes? Go and make me supper before I stop with all these niceties."

Backing away, Frances and Mary made their way to the kitchen while the grandfather from hell moaned some more. "Eyeballs make blooming good marbles, especially after you've given them a bit of spit and polish."

Feeling very pleased, Frances praised her friend, "Mary, you're quite good at hoodwinking."

Still trembling slightly, she answered, "For a moment I thought our goose was cooked."

"Really?"

Mary trembled some more, and sighed, "It felt like I had a stomach full of shooting stars exploding inside me."

Frances Fidget-Knickers waved her arms all around Mary and began to speak in her best witch's voice, "Crumbs and cranky, we're dabbling in hanky-panky."

"Yikes!" yelped Mary, mucking around. "I'm forever in your debt, oh great one."

The playful moment was ended by the washing machine shuddering to a stop.

"We weren't gone long, then?" questioned Mary, snapping out of her playful mood.

"I suppose not," said Frances, being herself again. "Magic time is different from normal time. What seems to take days in my world is only hours in this one."

"Just as well," blinked Mary, "or we would have no eyeballs left."

Frances held the bag up. "I'll be back in a minute – just got to hide these in my room."

Her friend stood there waiting and, true to her word, Frances was back in one minute flat. "I think we should press on," she insisted, unclipping the washing machine door.

Frances took one pair of trousers, along with one shirt, out of the drum. Pulling a wooden clothes horse open, she hung them over to dry. By the time Frances had cooked sausages, mashed potatoes, and mixed some gravy, the day had turned into evening. When the washing up was finally finished with, the two girls wandered off to the front room.

While they had been working away, there had been an unusual absence of Granddad Sprinkle-Tinkle.

This could only mean one thing.

The one thing that would keep him quiet all this time sat in the living room.

"What do you think your grandfather is doing?"

"Watching television."

"Anything in particular?"

"It's a programme called *Duff Stuff*," answered Frances, disinterested.

"Is it any good?"

"No, it's a load of old tosh, but it's my grandfather's favourite programme."

"What's it all about?"

"Basically, it's about trying to guess which antiques dealer has sold the duff item."

"That sounds rubbish."

As both girls entered the front room, they saw Granddad Sprinkle-Tinkle transfixed on a huge television screen. Wearing a pair of slippers and a dressing gown, he rocked back and forth.

"Do you want a drink, Granddad?" asked Frances.

"Shut up," moaned her grandfather, who was glued to the screen. "Can't you see it's coming to the best bit?"

Outside the cottage, a vehicle had stopped. A car door slammed shut and the gate opened. Footsteps walked up to the house.

Rearranging his tie, the unknown gentleman banged on the door and chuckled, "One born every minute – I should be able to take this lot for a pretty penny or two."

"See who that is and get rid of them," whinged Granddad Sprinkle-Tinkle.

"Oh, Granddad," gasped Frances Fidget-Knickers. "I mustn't answer the door when it's dark outside. Mummy told me never to do that. Mummy said it's because you never know who it might be at this time of night."

A second knock echoed out.

"Damned knocking," moaned her grandfather. "Why don't they just go away and be done with it? At least I'd get to watch me precious programme in peace."

The television blared out and the presenter was just about to announce the guilty person's name.

"Right then," said the presenter. "We come to the climax of the show."

A third knock echoed out.

Granddad Sprinkle-Tinkle, with an attitude of stubbornness, sat there refusing to budge. "I'm not moving, not now it's coming to the best part."

The television presenter continued, "Would the person responsible for this week's forgery please stand up and show the audience who did it."

By now, Granddad Sprinkle-Tinkle was so eager to know that he leant forwards and nearly fell out of the rocking chair. "I think it's that blighter with the moustache," he pointed. "Why he thinks his nose is so important that he needs to underline it with that hairy thing is beyond me."

Outside, the man who had been knocking spotted the doorbell. "Well, if they won't answer to my knocking, then I'll give this a try," he said, determinedly.

Suddenly, back in the front room, as the actor was about to stand up, the doorbell rang, the television switched itself off and all the lights went out.

"Blast it!" cried out Granddad Sprinkle-Tinkle. "Right at the best bit! Damn and blast them all! Whoever pressed that doorbell has caused this power cut! And now they're in for a piece of me mind!"

The whole cottage had fallen into complete darkness.

Frances softly spoke to Mary, "Where are you?"

"I'm right behind you," whispered Mary.

"It's spooky in the dark," said Frances. "Kind of mysterious when the lights go out."

With collywobbles in her tummy, Mary shuddered, "I can't see a blinking thing."

Frances Fidget-Knickers shouted through the darkness to her grandfather. "Granddad, we can't see a thing!"

133

"Never mind what you can't see!" yelled her grandfather. "What about me television programme? When I see who it is at that door, they're going to wish I'd never answered it!"

In the dark, everything seemed different. The two girls heard some odd squeaking and creaking noises. Granddad Sprinkle-Tinkle's hands made the sounds through getting up out of his rocking chair. The old man's eyes hadn't fully adjusted to the darkness. What happened next was this.

He took three pigeon steps forwards and tumbled over the coffee table. "Gawd help us!" he cried.

Then they heard a thump.

Getting back up, Granddad Sprinkle-Tinkle stepped onto some glossy magazines that had been left on the carpet. "AAAAGH!" he cried out, followed by a thud and the ruffling sounds of flying magazines.

Shakily, he got up again and stubbed his toe on a chair. "Ouch!" he shouted in pain, jumping up and down on one foot.

Due to the jumping up and down, he lost his balance once more and went crashing into the settee. "Heaven help us!" he screamed, as the settee smashed into the wall.

The room fell silent for a few seconds. The awkwardness of these few seconds seemed like a lifetime to the two girls.

"What's happening?" cried Frances Fidget-Knickers.

"Nothing I can't sort out!" shouted her slightly dazed grandfather, picking himself up and staggering to the front door.

Outside, the salesman was almost ready to give up. "I'm going to try it one last time and then I'm off and done with this place." He pushed the doorbell and nothing happened. "I suppose I'll have to knock, then."

For the fourth time, a knock on the door echoed through the cottage; it made an eerie echo in the darkness.

Frances and Mary stayed close to Granddad Sprinkle-Tinkle as he opened the front door.

Outside, a ray of moonlight illuminated the rutted dirt track, but the outer corners still remained mysterious and in the shadows.

Peering from behind her flustered grandfather, Frances could see a man standing on the porch step. He wore nice, shiny black shoes and a smart grey suit with a white shirt and a plain blue tie. In one hand he held a clipboard; with the other, he was tapping it with a pen.

Granddad Sprinkle-Tinkle was still a little dazed from his tumble.

"Good evening, Sir," smiled the stranger politely.

"Is it?" sniffed the old man, squinting through beady eyes.

"I should say so, Sir," answered the salesman.

"If you say so, then it must be," snorted Granddad Sprinkle-Tinkle, disgustedly.

"I'd like to introduce myself," said the gentleman. "I'm Mr Odourless and I work for the Gas Board."

"We ain't got no leaks," moaned Granddad Sprinkle-Tinkle, rubbing his head.

"No, Sir. Of course you haven't," agreed Mr Odourless. "I think you're misunderstanding me, Sir."

"If we ain't got no leaks, then why are you here?"

"That's a very good question, Sir," smiled Mr Odourless, clutching his clipboard with both hands. "We are in a position to offer you a reduction on your bills. When I say we, I mean the gas company of course. By having your gas and electricity supplied by one supplier, we are able to cut your bills by one hundred and fifty pounds per year. Now, Sir, what do you say to that?"

"How?" he asked, suspiciously.

By this time, Frances and Mary had plucked up some courage and stood either side of their horrid babysitter.

"Hello!" chirped Mr Odourless to both of them. "What are your names?"

"Never mind them," sniffed Granddad Sprinkle-Tinkle, his suspicion growing. "I want to know how you're going to save me that money. It sounds too good to be true and it sounds like a con, if you ask me."

"Well, Sir," said Mr Odourless, standing tall. With expert experience, he carried on. "It is not a con. I can assure you of that."

"Then how is it done?" asked Granddad Sprinkle-Tinkle, becoming a little agitated.

Mr Odourless stood his ground and explained, "The government, in its wisdom, has allowed the gas and electricity companies to compete in the supply of both electric and gas power. By purchasing your electricity and gas from us, we can pass on the cost-savings to our customers. By signing up with us today, we'll give you a loyalty bonus for your valued custom."

"So it's changes you're talking about?" asked Granddad Sprinkle-Tinkle, a temper tantrum brewing.

"Yes, that's right, Sir," smiled Mr Odourless, thinking at long last he might have a sale for his efforts. "And for the better, don't you agree?"

"Agree?" blasted out Granddad Sprinkle-Tinkle. "Ruddy governments! All they ever do is change things! Show me a politician and I'll smack them in the gob!"

The bellowing words forced Mr Odourless back onto the heels of his shoes. "Well, Sir!" he gasped in surprise. "I'm sorry if I've offended you, but I don't see how I have."

"Let me tell you something, Sonny Jim!" shrieked Granddad Sprinkle-Tinkle, whose face had gone redder than the ripest tomato. "Changes ain't no good for anybody!"

"Really, Sir," garbled the salesman. "I'm only doing my job."

"In my day, you young good-for-nothing excuse for a man, we did men's work!" roared Granddad Sprinkle-Tinkle. "We didn't do any of this pen-pushing, hairy-fairy stuff! Now clear off before I put me toe up your backside and sign your pants with compliments from me foot!"

"Good Heavens!" yelped Mr Odourless, making a hasty retreat. "Bless my soul! I've never been so humiliated in all my life!"

Granddad Sprinkle-Tinkle shook his fist in the air and shouted, "Ruddy hooligan, and good riddance to you!"

Scurrying back to his car, Mr Odourless mumbled to himself, "Well, I never, I've never met a more cantankerous old so-and-so in all my born days. You try and save someone their hard-earned cash and all you get in return is insults and abuse for your troubles."

The sound of a car engine fired up as Frances closed the door. Granddad Sprinkle-Tinkle wiggled the light switch as the car drove off. Suddenly, the power came back on. In the front room, the television blurted out.

"Right, you two!" snarled Granddad Sprinkle-Tinkle, still with his temper flaring. "You can go to bed and let me watch me programmes in peace!"

Still cursing, he moaned to himself, "If only I was twenty years younger, I'd have given him a punch in the guts!"

Frances and Mary rushed up the stairs and out of sight.

"Did you see that?" gasped Mary. "I thought your granddad was going to have a heart attack."

Frances Fidget-Knickers looked up to the ceiling and smiled, "House, was that you turning the power off?"

The cottage shook. "YES."

"Boy!" cried Mary. "What a surprise! Thanks, House!"

"YOU'RE WELCOME," replied House. "SWEET DREAMS AND GOODNIGHT."

"See you tomorrow, House," said Frances, getting ready for bed.

Mary walked around the room, undressing as she did so. "For a moment I thought it was Mrs Give-Us-A-Giggle."

Frances took off her clothes and folded them neatly. "Remember what she said – she didn't have the time."

Now ready for bed, they lay down and chatted.

"I wonder," sighed Mary Midget-Mouth, snuggling into the covers.

"Wonder about what?" asked Frances Fidget-Knickers, still wide awake.

"How good they will be," mumbled Mary, sleepily.

"Oh, the tricks," said Frances excitedly.

"Will they be as good as the stomach churner? Or the burning flame-thrower?" yawned Mary, beginning to doze off.

"Only tomorrow is going to tell us that," smiled Frances, jumping out of bed.

"What are you doing?" muttered Mary, half asleep.

"Just checking the bag with the Nibbling Nibblers in it," answered Frances, inspecting the bag before jumping back onto the mattress.

"Easy," moaned Mary. "I'm trying to go to sleep."

Frances jumped back out of bed.

"Now what are you doing?" asked Mary.

"Just checking if the soap is still there," she replied.

"Is it?"

"Yes," she answered, hopping back onto the mattress again.

"For goodness' sakes," said Mary, with a yawn. "Talk about living up to your name. Why don't you go to sleep?"

There was no reply and Mary turned around.

Frances Fidget-Knickers had fallen into a dreaming, peaceful sleep.

"I think I'll join you," smiled Mary Midget-mouth. "Goodnight."

CHAPTER 12

NIBBLING-NIBBLERS

The brand new day was trying to wake the two girls. A ray of piercing sunlight cut through the cracks between the curtains and shimmered over Frances Fidget-Knickers' and Mary Midget-Mouth's faces.

Frances stirred first, with sleepy, arm-flexing movements. "Mary, are you awake?"

"Get off!" she cried, kicking the bed covers. "You're not getting me!"

"Mary! You're dreaming."

Drowsily, she opened her eyes. "Thank goodness for that," Mary yawned. "It was horrible. I was dreaming that we'd been caught and Granddad Sprinkle-Tinkle was cooking us in a big boiling pot."

"That was nice of him, seeing that he never cooks," Frances chuckled, bouncing up and down on the bed.

"And I'd escaped …"

"Good for you," chirped Frances, jumping off the bed.

"He was chasing me, because I'd come back to rescue you."

"It's not going to be me who will need rescuing," she replied excitedly, "because today is going to be so much better than yesterday."

"Frances, where do you get all your energy from?" asked Mary, still half asleep.

"Maybe it's down to all the things I read," beamed Frances, flicking through a mountain of books. "By reading a good book from the comfort of my own bedroom, I can travel all over the world."

Mary sat up. Her friend's bedroom was stacked with more books than she could count. "I've never known anyone to read as much as you do."

"Look at this," yelped Frances, pulling out a book. "*Giggling Chop Busters* – I never stopped laughing all the time I was reading this one."

Mary stretched out her arms. "You read more than my parents do."

Putting the *Giggling Chop Busters* book down, Frances took another. "*Horror Stories that Give you Goose-Bumps* – I only read this one when I was with my mother and father, much too scary to read it on my own."

Mary's arms fell to the bed as she added, "And they are always reading."

Soon another book was held up. "*Chatting Sleepover Stories*," smiled Frances. "Some really juicy gossip in this one."

"Sounds interesting," Mary said with a yawn.

"And then there's this *Romantic Lip-Smacking Story*," grinned Frances, with an odd look. "It's a bit slobbery."

Getting up, Mary spluttered. "Yuck, I don't like the sound of that one!"

"I bet you'd like the sound of my grandfather getting his knickers in a twist?" she smiled happily.

"Do you think his clothes are dry?" asked Mary, looking over to where the Nibbling-Nibblers were.

Frances Fidget-Knickers quivered with excitement and picked up the paper bag.

It moved.

"I wonder what they do?" asked Mary.

"Shall we find out?" beamed Frances, a little more excited than before.

With a broad grin of pure pleasure, they played the game "follow-my-leader" all the way to the kitchen. Without a word spoken, they picked up the clothes from the clothes horse and got out the ironing board and iron.

Once the shirt and trousers had been ironed, Frances began to empty the Nibbling-Nibblers. "We mustn't get any on our hands," she muttered, concentrating really hard.

The tiny black Nibbling-Nibblers burrowed into the clothes and disappeared.

Then the clothes started to move.

"They must be searching for something to eat," suggested Mary, relishing the sight.

Just as the iron was turned off, in walked Granddad Sprinkle-Tinkle. "What are you doing with that iron?"

Thankfully, the garments stopped twitching as Frances replied smoothly, "I've just ironed your clothes for you, Granddad."

The old man's thoughts on ironing came out. "A waste of time," he sneered icily.

"You can't go around with creases in your clothes," Frances informed him.

The cold sneer had change, and from the sides of his mouth little bubbles appeared. "I never said you should," he grumbled disapprovingly.

"You implied it," said Frances, pushing her luck a little too far.

Granddad Sprinkle-Tinkle began spraying his spit bubbles about, while giving his granddaughter a dressing down. "That's where you're wrong. If you'd bothered to listen, I actually said 'a waste of time'."

Realising her mistake and, cleaning her face, she had to listen for the next thirty seconds of moaning.

"If you had waited a little longer I'd have explained why it's a waste of time, but no, you have to go sticking your nose in where it is not wanted. What I don't understand about ironing is this: why the stupid delinquents bother to perform such a task. When you iron clothes, me girl, what's the first thing you do with them?"

"Pick them up," answered Frances Fidget-Knickers, truthfully.

"After that, I meant, and don't get smart with me, girly," he said sternly. "Come on, what's the answer?"

Frances had no idea what he was getting at and just replied, "Fold them."

"So, there is a brain in there, after all?" said Granddad Sprinkle-Tinkle, sarcastically. "What's the second thing you do with them?"

Mary butted in. "Hang them on a coat hanger."

"I'll hang you on a coat hanger if you butt in once more when I'm talking to me granddaughter," retorted Granddad Sprinkle-Tinkle.

Rescuing her friend, Frances Fidget-Knickers quickly said, "Put them away."

"Wrong!" he snapped sharply.

"Carry them upstairs," added Mary, returning the favour of rescuing a friend in need.

"Wrong again!" he said sternly, and moaned on. "You put them on the side, iron another item and keep on going until the pile's a mountain high."

"My mother does that," smiled Mary.

Granddad Sprinkle-Tinkle didn't listen, as he moaned some more. "Then, you squash them all up by stacking them in cupboards. But low and behold, you don't stop there."

"Don't you?" asked Frances.

"No, you keep stacking and squashing the clothes until they've all got creases in again," grinned her grandfather. "So I was right when I said a waste of time, wasn't I?"

Frances and Mary said nothing.

"Lost the power to speak, have we?" sniffed Granddad Sprinkle-Tinkle. "In that case, I'll go and put me clothes on and you two can make me a nice mug of tea."

With that, he picked up the shirt and trousers. Storming off, he demanded, "You can half fill the mug with sugar this time. I need to keep me strength up after yesterday's performance. I'll be in me bedroom, so bring it up when it's ready."

When the mug of tea was ready, they made their way to Granddad Sprinkle-Tinkle's room and knocked on the door.

"Here's your tea, Granddad!" shouted Frances.

Behind the door, he had been practicing some nose-picking.

"Hurry up and bring it in here!" he shouted back.

As both girls walked in, a repulsive sight greeted them. Standing in front of the mirror, with his shirt and trousers back on, and with one finger up his nose, Granddad Sprinkle-Tinkle wiggled his finger furiously. "It's a big one," he declared.

Then he eased and teased and out popped his finger with a lump of snot on the end. "Got you," he smiled, holding the large green bogey up to the light as he began to examine it.

The nasal mucus glistened in the light and dangled for all to see.

"It's me best one ever!" After which, he became a snot-eater. "Yum!" he gulped.

Frances and Mary winced, their guts churning.

"Hurry up, I want to wash it down with me tea!" moaned Granddad Sprinkle-Tinkle. "You know I can't think straight in the morning without one."

Holding out the mug, Frances asked, "Where shall I put it?"

"Leave it on the side and get lost," he snapped.

Frances, along with Mary, staggered back to her bedroom while the Nibbling Nibblers waited.

"Eating bogeys is a disgusting habit," shuddered Mary, looking alarmed.

"His habits are repulsive at times," she agreed, giving her finger a wiggle and pretending to pull out a lump of snot.

"Frances, that's horrible," Mary winced.

Showing Mary her finger, Frances said, "Fancy some?"

Before Mary could answer, Granddad Sprinkle-Tinkle's words tore through her thoughts. "Frances!" he bellowed. "Something ain't right!"

As fast as they could run, both girls darted into his bedroom. "What's the matter, Granddad?" asked Frances, watching him wriggle all over the place. "You're acting very peculiar again!"

"Something ain't right with me clothes!" cried her grandfather. "What have you both been doing to them?"

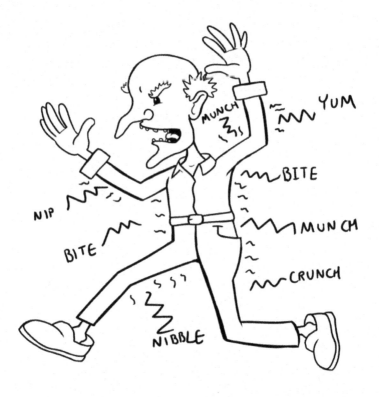

With a convincing bewildered look, she answered, "I only washed them with the new washing powder because the old packet ran out."

"Blasted washing powder!" he snapped.

"Do you think you're allergic to the new washing powder?" asked Mary.

"Changes, changes, changes!" he moaned.

Turning to Frances, Mary casually chatted on, with a secret wink of her eye. "Once, I saw this programme where someone had changed their eating habits, and all their hair and teeth fell out."

They turned back to face Granddad Sprinkle-Tinkle, who was doing a funny little jig.

"Damned new-fangled changes!" he itched.

"They're no good for anyone!" he scratched.

"Especially me!" he wriggled.

"Goodness!" gasped Frances Fidget-Knickers. "Do you think there's something wrong with the washing powder?"

Granddad Sprinkle-Tinkle was too busy hopping, scratching and jumping around the bedroom to answer.

Mary continued talking. "On this programme, they also said that sometimes if you haven't stored groceries properly, they get infested with little bugs."

The old man's ears pricked up. "Bugs, that's what it is!" he squealed, agreeing with Mary. "You can bet your bottom dollar that's what it is, alright!"

The Nibbling-Nibblers were just getting started. It was just about to get a lot worse for the awful grandfather. First they started to bite into the old man's eyebrows. When they had finished, they crawled from his brow to his head, and munched on what very little hair he had left. After they had eaten up all of his hair, the Nibbling-Nibblers began to sink their tiny, razor-sharp teeth into his scalp.

Wave after wave of irritating feelings penetrated deep down into his pores, with dreadful consequences. And with that, the worst grandfather of all time shot from the room.

"AAAAAAGH!" he screamed. "I'm alive with creepy-crawlies!"

Shooting downstairs, he screamed some more. "I've got ants in me pants!"

Jetting around the hallway in an uncontrolled panic, he yelled, "And it's getting worse!"

"Granddad!" shouted Frances, running down the stairs with Mary by her side. "You're acting very strange!"

Frances and Mary stood there admiring the trick, but then a feeling of astonishment took over. Something unexpected started to happen. A complex process of change began.

At first, Granddad Sprinkle-Tinkle slowed down and gradually came almost to a standstill.

Then he stopped.

"That's very odd," said Mary Midget-Mouth. "Is that supposed to happen?"

From behind them, a voice spoke, "No, me dears."

"Mrs Give-Us-A-Giggle!" gasped Frances Fidget-Knickers, spinning around at the same time as Mary.

The white witch stood there looking over their heads, the magic of time happening right before them. "Thought I'd make some time and give you a helping hand," she smiled approvingly.

"Are you doing that to Granddad Sprinkle-Tinkle?" asked Mary, admiringly.

"Of course I am, me dear," she answered. "Making time slow down is a very tricky spell. It took me a bit of time to work it out."

The white witch stopped. Then she smiled. The smile grew into a chuckle. Then she started to laugh.

"Get it? Bit of time, me dears. That's a funny one! Quite by accident, I might add."

Dazzled by her infectious laugh, Frances and Mary giggled too.

Mrs Give-Us-A-Giggle stopped laughing and said, "Let me see, by now the Nibbling-Nibblers should be at their worst. I'll just put time back to where it should be. He won't see or hear me because I've put a blocking spell on him."

Instantly, everything was back to normal and Granddad Sprinkle-Tinkle was acting like an insane person, ripping at his clothes. "There's little itsy-bitsy bugs in me clothes! And what's more, they're not agreeing with me skinnnnn!"

Frances, Mary and the white witch watched on, as the old man went dancing and prancing, hopping and bopping, round and round in circles.

He turned every which way there was to turn.

His arms darted and flashed over his tormented body.

"Suffering suffragettes!" he squealed in agony. "Don't just stand there, get over here and give me a hand!"

There was a look of real horror on Frances Fidget-Knickers' face.

"Don't worry about the Nibbling-Nibblers," said Mrs Give-Us-A-Giggle. "Once they have the scent of their victim, they won't eat anything else."

With that bit of information stored, Frances asked, "What do you want me to do, Granddad?"

"Don't ask stupid questions!" screamed her infested grandfather. "Just get over here with Mary and scratch me back!"

By now, the wicked old man did not know which way to turn. Both girls did as they were told, and began to scratch Granddad Sprinkle-Tinkle's back.

"Harder!" he cried, in a shrill tone that felt like it would split their heads open. "Can't you do it any harder?"

Frances and Mary dug their fingernails in and tore at his back. "Is that any better?" spluttered Frances.

"Harder!" cried his reply.

Mary pushed down with all her might and asked, "Does that feel better?"

Granddad Sprinkle-Tinkle just screamed out, "Harder!"

"We're doing it as hard as we can!" gasped Frances Fidget-Knickers. "Maybe you need a bath?"

"How dare you!" yelled her grandfather. "How dare you say a thing like that!"

"It's only a bath, Granddad," gulped Frances, as her hands scratched at his body.

Crying out in pain he informed them, "You know I only have one bath a year! And that's not for another four months!"

"But Granddad," cried Frances, almost out of breath, "it might be the only way to stop you from itching so much!"

Mary quickly added, "Bugs don't like water. It said so, on that programme I watched the other day."

"Blinking changes!" shouted Granddad Sprinkle-Tinkle. "No good comes from blimmin' changes! I suppose I'll have to have two baths this year!"

With that, he rushed into the bathroom, slamming the door behind him.

"Well, me dears," smiled Mrs Give-Us-A-Giggle, "I almost forgot to tell you – Nibbling-Nibblers do funny things when they come into contact with water. Oh my, look at the time. Can't stop, got to get back, I've got customers waiting. Bye bye, me dears."

Then she faded away, writing something down on a small notepad while she did so.

"What did she mean about the Nibbling-Nibblers and water?" asked Mary.

Frances just shrugged her shoulders. "We'll soon find out."

CHAPTER 13

A SHOCKING EXPERIENCE

Behind the bathroom door came the sounds of a crazed panic. Frances Fidget-Knickers pressed her ear against the wooden barrier. The inner ear inside her skull became more acute and listening-efficient, the harder she concentrated.

"He's turning on the bath taps."

"What's he doing now?"

"I can't tell, there's too much noise," she answered, pressing harder against the door.

"Look! There's a note on the floor!" cried out Mary, spotting some paper on the landing and running over to it. "It's got your name on it."

Frances stopped listening. She knew instantly whom it was from, and took the note, and then she opened it.

The note spoke. "Hello, me dears. I forgot to tell you, I've put a memory-blocking spell on Granddad Sprinkle-Tinkle. So, whatever happens, he won't remember a thing, and you'll be in the clear. We wouldn't want him punishing you and your friend, now, would we, me dears?"

Suddenly, the note crumbled into dust, fell to the floor and vanished.

"Why can't all letters be like that?" Mary Midget-Mouth sighed. "It would save me a load of homework in Mr Do-It-Again's English class."

"I like him, he's really nice," smiled Frances.

"He's okay, but all he ever tells me is 'Mary Midget-Mouth, what do you call this? Not good enough' young lady, do it again'."

A cry of frustration broke out from inside the bathroom. "Oh, blast it! Where's the soap gone!"

"Granddad!" shouted Frances. "I've put it in the bathroom cabinet!"

"I'm not getting it!" called out her horrid grandfather. "I'm in the bath and I refuse to get out because I'm feeling much better! You'll have to come in and get it for me!"

"But, Granddad, you've got nothing on!" cried Frances, looking at Mary and making an awkward face. "Mummy is always telling me never to go in the bathroom when someone else is in there!"

"Shut up with your complaining!" he shouted. "I've still got me pants on!"

"Haven't you locked the door?" asked Frances.

"No," answered the old man, "so get in here at once!"

"What would Mummy say?" called Frances.

"If you don't get in here and I have to get out of this nice, relaxing bath," shouted her grandfather, "then I'll put your head down the toilet and flush some sense into you!"

Frances Fidget-Knickers held Mary's hand and took a deep breath. Leaning against the door, they went in. There in the bath sat Granddad Sprinkle-Tinkle, with just a pair of pants on. In the bath with him sat the Nibbling-Nibblers, nesting on the top of his head.

"Hurry up, child, before I lose me patience with you," he moaned.

Frances got the magic bar of soap and handed it over. Once unwrapped, it sat gleaming with mischief in the old man's hand.

"Here," sniffed Granddad Sprinkle-Tinkle, "you can take the wrapper."

Getting ready to leave Frances said, "We'll just go and throw the rubbish away."

"You'll do no such thing," he insisted. "Stay where I can see you."

152

From the moment that the soap was dipped in the bathwater and Granddad Sprinkle-Tinkle started to wash, it began to happen. Lightning flashes sparked out and exploded.

Astounded, he cried out, "What's happening?"

Flashes and flares kept sparking out.

"I hate it, I hate it, I hate it!" he shouted over and over again.

Frances and Mary were mesmerised by it all.

Splashing some water, Granddad Sprinkle-Tinkle rolled up into a little ball. "It's unbearable!" he protested.

Suddenly, all the sparks and flashes stopped. Then a single flash of exploding light shot out. "Unbearable?" boomed a voice so chilling that it would have frozen hell over.

"Now I'm hearing things!" cried the horrid old man, scared.

The exploding light turned into a face. "So you think you're hard done by?" boomed the face.

"Me eyes!" Granddad Sprinkle-Tinkle cried in shock. "I'm going round the twist! Now me eyes are seeing things as well!"

"Quiet, you horrible little man!" roared the face.

"I've lost me marbles!" cried Granddad Sprinkle-Tinkle. Confused, he turned to Frances and Mary. "Can you see it?"

"See what?" said Frances, playing along with the trick.

"Is there something wrong?" asked Mary.

The quivering old man closed his eyes so tight that not even a splash of water could get in. "I'm getting old before me time," he moaned. "Next thing you know I'll be losing me good looks."

Shakily, he opened his eyes to see if the face was still there.

Unfortunately for him, it was.

"You-good-for-nothing excuse for a grandfather!" bellowed the face. "Look at you! You're old and past it!"

"That's it," he mumbled. "You're not really there. It's all in me mind."

With that, Frances and Mary watched Granddad Sprinkle-Tinkle punch out and hit the face in front of him.

"Ouch!" her grandfather cried out in amazement. "You're real!"

"So you want to play rough?" snarled the face, growing a body and two arms. "They call me the Widow Maker, you old fleabag!"

A hand snapped out and, with one arm, Granddad Sprinkle-Tinkle was hanging upside down.

Eagerly, the Nibbling-Nibblers were getting ready.

"Help!" he cried, from his upside-down position. "Someone call the police!"

Frances and Mary just watched in awe.

"Listen up, you old worm-infested excuse for a man!" blasted the Widow Maker, beginning to shake him up and down. "I'm here to teach you a lesson!"

"Dial nine, nine, nine!" cried Granddad Sprinkle-Tinkle, as his head went in and out of the bathwater.

The Nibbling-Nibblers reacted violently with the water. Just like a New Year's party after the stroke of midnight, the room was filled with explosions.

Snap, sizzle, pop, bang – the Nibbling-Nibblers exploded.

"Ouch, me head!" cried out Granddad Sprinkle-Tinkle, as one of the exploding Nibbling-Nibblers crashed into him.

From all angles, the Nibbling-Nibblers were attacking. "Ouch! Ouch! Ouch!" shouted the nasty old man repeatedly.

"Shampoo!" cried the Widow Maker, in the midst of the fireworks display.

"No!" screamed Granddad Sprinkle-Tinkle. "I don't like it!"

The Widow Maker clicked his fingers and the bathroom cabinet door flew open. Out floated the bottle of shampoo into his free hand.

Frances decided the thought inside her head was too good to stay there, so she said, "If he leaves him upside down for long enough, then everything will fall back into place, like it used to be."

Mary laughed.

Frances giggled.

And the Widow Maker carried on. "You're a sorry, ancient bag of bones!" he shouted. "I wonder if you rattle!"

Mary stopped laughing and watched.

Frances stopped giggling and did the same.

The Widow Maker began to shake Granddad Sprinkle-Tinkle like a baby's rag doll.

"Stop it!" he gabbled.

"You can't even do that right!" hollered the Widow Maker, shaking him even harder, as the Nibbling-Nibblers carried on with their attack.

"I don't care what I can't do!" the old man squirmed. "Just stop it and put me down!"

"I'll put you down, alright, you old mongrel," smiled the Widow Maker, dropping him on his head.

"Ouch!" cried Granddad Sprinkle-Tinkle, turning the right way up.

There was no time for the old man to rub his head before more Nibbling-Nibblers exploded.

Pop, whizz, bang, they went.

There was no time for Granddad Sprinkle-Tinkle to take cover, as the Widow Maker had already grabbed the horrid man by the scruff of his neck. "Get off! Leave me alone!" he squirmed.

"I'll rub some shampoo in, to make it feel better," the Widow Maker continued smoothly, squeezing the shampoo out.

The Nibbling-Nibblers continued the bombardment.

Pop, whizz, bang, bang, they fired off in a blinding light of exploding rockets.

"Me eyes!" screamed Granddad Sprinkle-Tinkle.

"Last time I looked, you still had two," smiled the maker of death, washing the shampoo all over his face.

Still, the Nibbling-Nibblers carried on with their barrage.

Bang, bang, pop, whizz, they went on exploding.

"Me eyes have got shampoo in them!" squealed Granddad Sprinkle-Tinkle.

"That's really painful," shuddered Frances.

"Not half," agreed Mary.

"It's not just me eyes!" cried out the old man, as the Nibbling-Nibblers went thwack, wallop, whack, into his body.

"That must really hurt," laughed the Widow Maker. "Let's rub some more shampoo in."

"AA-WA-WAL!" cried Granddad Sprinkle-Tinkle. "It does, quick, wash it out!"

"If you say so," said the Widow Maker, turning the old man upside down again. He dunked his head in and out of the water. "Is that better?"

"I hate it, I hate it, I hate it!" Granddad Sprinkle-Tinkle spluttered. "Baths are a blinking annoyance!"

"There's no need to worry – the shampoo will be gone in a minute," said the Widow Maker, pushing him in and out of the bathwater like a plunger.

"That's what I'm worried about!" coughed the old man. "When you stop with all this, what will you be doing next?"

"Nothing," bellowed the trick, as it disappeared.

Instantly, Granddad Sprinkle-Tinkle fell in a heap and the bathwater splashed everywhere. He sat there wiping his eyes, without a clue in the world as to what had just happened.

The powerful blocking spell had done its work.

"Right, you two," said Granddad Sprinkle-Tinkle, regaining his horrid attitude. "I don't want a word out of you. That way, I can get on with washing these bugs away."

Squelching a flannel and rubbing his skin with the soap, another shocking experience began to occur.

Something extraordinary and fantastic oozed out of the soap. The shade was spectacular. It was brilliant, illuminating and very, very bright.

"Granddad!" cried Frances. "I think there's something wrong with the soap!"

"I said no talking!" snapped her grandfather.

"But, Granddad— "

"Are you wanting punishments?"

"No, Granddad," Frances answered quietly.

"I'm sorry to hear that," sniffed the horrid old man. "Any more interruptions and you'll get a thick ear for your trouble."

Frances and Mary gazed in disbelief at the stupendous sight unfolding in front of them. For the next few minutes, the girls watched, flabbergasted, with Granddad Sprinkle-Tinkle totally oblivious to what was happening to him.

When the body-washing was finished with, he grumbled, "Go and get me a pair of your father's shorts. Come on, hurry yourselves — I want to get dried and dressed in privacy."

So off they went.

The stinging in his eyes was easing. They were starting to become less painful. But Granddad Sprinkle-Tinkle's vision still remained a little blurred. Unknown to him, with a smothering completeness, the soap had weaved its magic.

Clothes in hand, Frances returned with Mary, leaving a pair of cream-coloured shorts hanging from the bathroom door handle. "There – hanging over the handle, Granddad!" she shouted.

The door opened ever so slightly. A hand came out, then the shorts were gone along with the hand. Two seconds later, Granddad Sprinkle-Tinkle came out wearing just a pair of light cream shorts.

Frances and Mary screamed out in horror, for the sight in front of them was truly shocking.

158

"G-G-Granddad, y-y-you're g-g-green!" stuttered Frances Fidget-Knickers, pretending to be surprised.

Also pretending to be surprised, Mary Midget-Mouth gasped.

"Eh?" shouted Granddad Sprinkle-Tinkle, wiggling a finger in his ear. "What did you say? I can't hear a thing with all this water in me lughole!"

Frances carried on with her ruse and stuttered some more. "I-I-I said, you're g-g-green!"

"Don't talk nonsense, girly," grumbled Granddad Sprinkle-Tinkle, "I've just had a bath."

Mary came in on the stuttering. "B-B-But you are green!" she gawked, then adding normally, "If you don't believe us, you should take a look at yourself in the mirror!"

With the intention of doing just that, he marched off.

The girls followed him to the only full-length mirror in the cottage. Now in the master bedroom, the old man stood and faced the reflecting glass.

"Let me see," he mumbled.

Squinting through bloodshot eyes, he gradually focused on his reflection. "I can't see what all the fuss is about," he huffed.

Slowly at first, the image in front of him came into focus. "Nothing wrong here," he sniffed.

Now the image started to make sense in his brain. "Wait a minute," he gasped in horror. And now, with his mouth open and gaping in disbelief, he was flummoxed. Like a pulverising blow to the head, his brain had been crippled from the shock.

After a torrent of panicking mumbo-jumbo, he started to make sense and screamed out, "I'm green! Not just any green! But a brilliant and illuminating green! Heavens above, I'm scarred for life!"

The sight was truly captivating. It was a wondrous vision, thoroughly enjoyed by Frances and Mary. "I tried to tell you, Granddad, but you wouldn't listen."

With trembling movements, the illuminating old man panicked. "What am I to do? I can't go around looking like a giant frog for the rest of me life! I'm doomed, I tell you! Cursed to look like a brightly coloured lizard for the rest of me days!"

Mary said in fascination, "My father cleans stuff with turpentine. He swears it's the best thing he knows for cleaning out things."

Jumping on Mary's idea, Frances said to her grandfather, "Do we have any turpentine in the garage?"

"Questions, questions and more blinking questions," he whined. "At a time like this, you expect me to decorate? There's just no peace for your old granddad. What have I done to deserve a fate like this?"

Then Frances Fidget-Knickers suggested. "What about petrol?"

At that instance, Granddad Sprinkle-Tinkle stopped moaning. Now listening to his granddaughter, he took great interest in what she was saying.

"Daddy uses it to wash off grease, you know, from his hands after tinkering with the car."

With the sudden interest in juice, that makes cars run, Granddad Sprinkle-Tinkle cried out, "By dinkums! You might be onto something there! Your father keeps a tin of petrol in the garage for emergencies! And right now this is an emergency that requires immediate attention!"

Not waiting any longer, he was off like the clappers and flew from the bedroom. Flying down the stairs and out of the back door, he raced along to the garage. Frances and Mary had a job to keep up. By the time they entered the garage, Granddad Sprinkle-Tinkle was already searching through the tins of leftover paints.

"White undercoat, non-drip gloss," he muttered. Pushing his hands in and out, he moved the tins aside. "It can't be up here – it's got to be somewhere else," he stressed.

Then he spotted it. "That will do! It's not petrol, but white spirit should get it off," he smiled. "After all, it works on paintbrushes."

Tipping the container of white spirit above his head, the liquid came gurgling out and showered over him. The garage was filled with vapours. The vapours really kicked up a stench. They got right up Frances and Mary's noses.

"It's not working!" cried out Granddad Sprinkle-Tinkle. "Where's the damned petrol instead?"

"There it is, Granddad!" said Frances, holding her nose.

"Where?" he coughed.

"Over there, by the lawnmower!" choked Frances.

Snatching the petrol can quickly, he unscrewed the top. Holding it above his head, a shower of engine juice came gushing out.

The toxic, eye-watering fumes mixed with the white spirit was enough to take their breath away.

Frances gasped.

Mary coughed.

"It's still not ruddy working!" spluttered Granddad Sprinkle-Tinkle, standing in a puddle of obnoxious liquid. "I'm doomed! I'm condemned! I'll be green for all me born days yet to come!"

Frances and Mary smiled at one another.

With a violent bout of anger brewing, his mumbles spilled over and into a tremendous mouthful of cursing words. "I'll have him! I'll bash him! I'll even ruddy smash him!" bellowed the stench ridden old man, waving his arms around like a man gone mad.

The two girls shuffled back.

Meaner than a rattlesnake, he shook with rage and then went totally ballistic. "Wait 'til I see that delivery man! I'll knock him into next week! And if he comes back after that, I'll kick him to kingdom come as well!"

It was amazing how fast the petrol and white spirit evaporated. Only the stench remained, and clung to the old man's body. The rest of the day he sat in his rocking chair, smelling to high heaven and grumbling.

Now in the sanctuary of Frances Fidget-Knickers' bedroom, the two girls chatted.

"I thought that was the trick when that head appeared," said Mary excitedly.

"Me too," smiled Frances, closing her door. "Isn't she fantastic?"

In her excitement, Mary ran over to the bed and dived on it. With her mind distracted, she asked, "Who?"

"Mrs Give-Us-A-Giggle," answered Frances happily.

"Not half," Mary agreed.

The cottage shook. "SHE'S THE MOST POWERFUL WHITE WITCH THERE IS," House said knowledgeably.

"House," beamed Frances, staring at the ceiling. "We did it for you."

"THANK YOU," replied House. "YOU CARRY ON CHATTING, I'VE GOT THINGS TO DO."

After House had seemingly disappeared, Mary sighed. "If only there was more time. The weekend seems to have passed by so quickly. I bet Mrs Give-Us-A-Giggle has a million more tricks up her sleeve."

When the evening meal had been eaten, and everything was tidied away, they all sat in the front room.

It was just before eight in the evening that a message came through. Frances and Mary sat opposite Granddad Sprinkle-Tinkle.

Granddad Sprinkle-Tinkle sat next to a little red telephone. It started to ring. "You can answer it," he insisted.

Frances trotted over and picked up the telephone receiver. "Hello," she said, politely

Mary Midget-Mouth and Granddad Sprinkle-Tinkle listened in as the conversation started to unfold.

Suddenly, Frances Fidget-Knickers' voice changed, as she recognised the person talking on the other end. "Mummy, it's you."

Her grandfather glanced over.

Glancing over to her grandfather, she said to him, "Granddad, its Mummy and Daddy."

"So what?" he mumbled.

Frances smiled at Mary and glowed with excitement as she repeated her mother's words. "You had a smashing time!" And then she shouted at her grandfather, "Mummy has had a wonderful holiday, Granddad!"

"More than some of us have had," he muttered, turning away with a sniff.

"Really?" cried Frances, looking straight at her grandfather. "I don't mind, Mummy. I really don't, honest, Mummy."

Granddad Sprinkle-Tinkle looked back at Frances. "Now what?" he moaned.

"Mummy loved it so much she's decided to stay another week," she told her granddad.

"Some people have all the luck," he grumbled.

"Bye bye, Mummy, give my love to Daddy!" called Frances down the telephone.

Just before Frances Fidget-Knickers replaced the receiver, she said to her mother, "Of course I'll be alright. Yes, I'm sure, Mummy. Not to worry."

And then the last thing she said, with a sly glance at Granddad Sprinkle-Tinkle, said it all. "Of course I'll look after Granddad until you get home."

Spot the difference

Just for fun, there are six things different with these pictures, can you find them all.

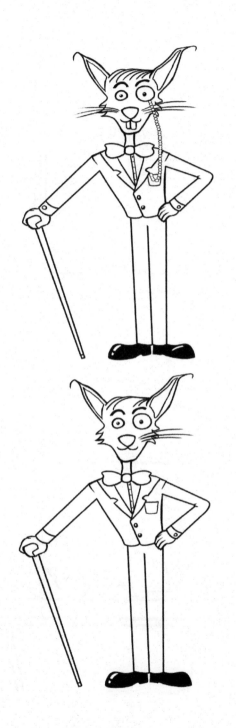

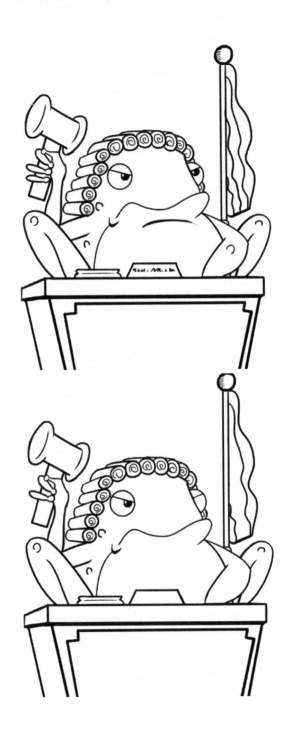

Lightning Source UK Ltd.
Milton Keynes UK
UKOW04f0943111017
310795UK00001B/24/P